As a child, **ANNA CLEARY** loved reading so much that during the midnight hours she was forced to read with a torch under the bedcovers, to lull the suspicions of her sleep-obsessed parents. From an early age she dreamed of writing her own books in a stone cottage by the sea, wearing a velvet smoking jacket and sipping sherry, like Somerset Maugham.

In real life she became a schoolteacher, and her greatest pleasure was teaching children to write beautiful stories.

A little while ago, she and one of her friends made a pact to each write the first chapter of a romance novel on their school holidays. From writing her very first line, Anna was hooked, and she gave up teaching to become a full-time writer. She now lives in Brisbane, Australia, with her daughter and a deeply sensitive and intelligent cat. She prefers champagne to sherry, and loves music, books, four-legged people, trees, movies and restaurants.

MY TALL DARK GREEK BOSS

ANNA CLEARY

~ IN BED WITH THE BOSS ~

HARLEQUIN®

TORONTO • NEW YORK • LONDON
AMSTERDAM • PARIS • SYDNEY • HAMBURG
STOCKHOLM • ATHENS • TOKYO • MILAN • MADRID
PRAGUE • WARSAW • BUDAPEST • AUCKLAND

ISBN-13: 978-0-373-82077-1
ISBN-10:   0-373-82077-1

MY TALL DARK GREEK BOSS

First North American Publication 2008.

This edition published by arrangement with Harlequin Books S.A.

® and TM are trademarks of the publisher. Trademarks indicated with ® are registered in the United States Patent and Trademark Office, the Canadian Trade Marks Office and in other countries.

www.eHarlequin.com

Printed in U.S.A.

MY TALL DARK
GREEK BOSS

For Jenny

PROLOGUE

Samos Stilakos leaned his tall frame against the bar. Displeasure darkened his stern, handsome face. Why, he wondered, had he allowed himself to be persuaded into attending the Sirius Bank's Annual Masked Ball? He was a financier, not some show-business scout. And where the hell was this woman who was supposed to be his hostess?

Nothing they showed him now could save them, anyway, he thought, strafing the throng of colourful characters with his dark gaze. Least of all a staff function at a beach hotel.

As often at celebrations, the urge came over him to stride from the room, head for the airport and fly. Somewhere. Anywhere. Some deserted isle, or a snow-capped mountain in Peru, where the only music was the rush of wind. Anywhere free from this noise.

He glowered at the ballroom's lavish decorations. For a bank about to plunge straight to the bottom of Sydney Harbour, no expense had been spared. Under the glitter of the chandeliers, the Sirius staff were switched into party mode, and seethed with an excitement bordering on delirium.

Exactly what his ex-wife would have loved, Sam brooded, watching a scarlet-cloaked Romeo cavorting with a laughing, shrieking woman on the dance floor. His sensuous mouth hardened.

A pity they weren't tuned into the reality facing their bank.

An adventurous Catwoman swayed out of the mêlée and reached up to put her hands on his shoulders. 'Dance, gorgeous?' Through the slits in her mask her eyes gleamed with allure.

Sexy, he had to admit, but did the bank's directors really think he'd succumb to such a ploy? 'I don't dance,' he said, politely removing her clinging hands. She murmured something about Greek gods *any time* before she undulated her way back into the party crowd, but Sam didn't catch it.

He wondered if that had been the purpose of the courtesy suite they'd pressed on him. Was this woman they'd told him to expect intended as a sweetener? It wouldn't be the first time he'd been offered such an enticement.

They should have done their homework, he grimaced. If he did decide to rescue the ailing bank, they'd learn.

In the Stilakos Organisation ethics were everything.

'Sorry. Sorry about that, Mr Stilakos.' Stephen Fletcher, Sirius's portly Senior HR Executive, was unconvincingly attired as a gangster. 'I don't know what can be keeping Ellie.' He flashed Sam a quick, nervous grin. 'Are you enjoying the party?'

Sam stared incredulously at the rotund executive. 'Is this how you usually do business at Sirius? You invite potential investors to your staff parties?'

Fletcher gazed up at him with an earnest intensity. 'No, no. Not at all. Only you. We wanted you to see for yourself… We wanted you to *understand* the Sirius Staff Policy. At Sirius we want our team to *work*.' He thumped the bar to make the word stick. 'That, we firmly believe, means giving our folk ample opportunity to *play*.'

Sam's mouth twisted with sudden humour. 'Seriously? You thought this—' he swept one lean, bronzed hand towards the exuberant throng of assorted harem girls and Ned Kellys '—this would convince me to bail out your bank?'

'Well, not me alone. It was someone else who suggested showing you the *human face* of the Sirius Bank.' Fletcher's fist connected emphatically with the bar. 'She thought that your seeing the *actual people* involved—' thump, thump '—in a *personal* sense... The wonderful men and women whose livelihoods are *on the line*—' For an alarming second his hyperactive fist came close to seizing Sam's lapel. 'If you could only key into the real issues of *sincere human beings*, and try to *forget* the bottom line...'

Sam listened in thunderstruck amazement. No wonder the Sirius Bank was in trouble. What bank tried to operate with this folksy creed?

He lifted his brows in amusement. 'And whose was the great brain who thought I might be overwhelmed by the personal charms of your workforce?'

Fletcher saw unexpected warmth lightening the forbidding expression of the bank's rich suitor, as if the sun had been there all the time and was about to break through. For the first time since he'd met Samos Stilakos, he knew a ray of hope.

'Ellie,' he replied eagerly. 'Ellie O'Dea. Your hostess. She's one of my staff. You'll like her, I'm sure. Charming. Charming girl. And a real looker, too. You won't be disappointed, I asssure you. She's been briefed and she's all prepared for you. She must be here by now. Ellie's not usually late— Hang on!'

He stood on tiptoe to scan the milling crowd, trying to pick Ellie out from among the fancifully garbed women, then turned and collided with black ice in Sam Stilakos's eyes. He felt the very breath freeze in his lungs.

Stilakos looked down at him from his considerable height, the essence of polished courtesy, though his smile chilled Fletcher to the core. 'I appreciate your assistance.' The clipped precision of his deep, cool voice injected an icy sliver between Fletcher's ribs. 'Fletcher, wasn't it? I've seen all I need. Don't let me keep you from your celebration.'

Fletcher shook his head in consternation. 'But—but I hoped I could introduce you—' With the cold realisation of defeat he met Samos Stilakos's unforgiving gaze. He hovered for a moment, then, his shoulders slumped, edged away.

Sam watched him go, then turned to survey the ball, disillusion in his heart.

Once the challenge of the Sirius Bank would have appealed to him. Its sad market performance and falling profits made it as attractive a proposition for the Stilakos Organisation as he could remember. He could buy it for a song, give it a drastic structural shake-up, and, with an exhilarating measure of risk, take it straight to the top of the tree. If its indulgent staff culture didn't hold it back. And if—

Face it. If he weren't so *bored*.

Lately his zest for winning against the odds seemed to have blunted. What he needed, he mused, was one damned good reason to buy the bank beyond making money.

A voluptuous Cleopatra spotted him and started an unsteady progress towards him. Not tonight, sweetheart, Sam thought grimly. What he wanted, what he needed...

An indefinable longing surged through him, reminding him of the nights of his youth. Nights when there'd been magic in the air, and mystery in a woman's face. Where had it all gone? All at once the noise, heat and activity reached an unbearable pitch. He loosened his tie and looked about for the nearest exit.

In the hall beyond the ballroom heavy curtains beckoned. He shoved some unsecured balloons aside, and threaded his way through the throng. If he could just get away from the relentless carnival atmosphere...

Thank God the doors weren't locked. He stepped out into the soft dark, onto a long balcony, and was met with a wave of fresh, salty air. The door closed behind him, and instantly the hullabaloo was cut.

It took him a moment to adjust. Still early in the season, the night was cool, but the promise of summer carried on the breeze like a woman's perfume.

He strolled over to the rail. Across the street from the hotel was the beach walk, and beyond it the vast, black heaving space of the sea. A gentle susurration spoke caressingly to him of the surf, curling itself up on the dark beach below the sea wall.

Flexing the muscles in his powerful arms and shoulders, he breathed in deeply, as if to inhale some energising essence from the brilliant night sky. He watched the moon's flickering progress under a few wispy clouds, then started as a small sound alerted him to a presence.

Something. Or someone.

He stiffened, every muscle on the alert, and searched the dim balcony. In the furthest corner he thought he could make out a figure. He strained his eyes against the dark. The moon chose that moment to peep through, and something took shape that resembled a human form.

'Hello?' he said, taking a few steps that way.

At the sound of his voice the figure stilled, as though frozen to the wall. Intrigued, he began to walk towards the mysterious presence. Who would be lurking outside in the dark at this hour, unless they were up to no good?

'Whoever you are,' he said firmly, 'you'd better come forward and introduce yourself.'

The form moved, and at once he recognised it as being female. 'Don't come any closer,' a feminine voice said sharply.

He stopped in his tracks. 'Why not?'

There was a moment of silence, then she said in a strangled voice, 'Because you're invading my personal space. Now back off.'

He grinned to himself. 'Oh, come on. You can't claim an entire public balcony as your personal space.' Curiosity aroused, he strained his eyes to make her out. There was something strangely unearthly about the woman's pale form, like a wraith seen through a mist.

At that moment the moon burst from behind a cloud, drenching the balcony in its silvery glow. The breath caught in his throat, halting him to the spot.

She was an ethereal vision, gowned in shimmering white. An angel. A moon nymph. Beneath some glittery ornament, her long hair fell almost to her waist, and her face was strangely shadowed. A sensation of unreality, almost of magic, swept through him, as if he'd stepped into some childhood fairy tale.

'There's no need to come any closer,' she flung at him, a repressive note in her voice. 'I'm not in the mood for a chat, so you might as well stay right where you are.'

Sam laughed, his blood quickening. 'I'm not much of a one for small talk, myself.'

He felt rather than saw the glare from her shadowed eyes, and as he moved closer realised that of course she was wearing a mask.

'Now let me see…' He smiled as he took in the full extent of her slender, moonlit form, deliciously outlined in clinging satin. She held her hands folded at her breast, while on the ground beside her feet a couple of large, silver-trimmed wings reposed limply against the wall. 'What are you? An angel?' he enquired, smiling, then, recognising her crown, 'Ah, of course. You must be the Fairy Queen. What's her name? Titania, isn't it?'

Trapped in her worst nightmare, Ellie O'Dea clung tightly to her frail bodice. As her big, masculine discoverer drew nearer, she racked her brains for a way to get rid of him without betraying her gown's fragile coverage of her vulnerable breasts.

'Well done,' she said. 'Anyway, it was great to meet you. My boyfriend will be back soon, so don't feel you have to wait.'

She held her breath. The mention of her boyfriend—just supposing she still had one and he hadn't dumped her in favour of Antarctica—might have worked, as for the moment the stranger remained where he was. He was tall, at least six-three, she guessed, *big*, and though in the dark his face was shadowy, its lean planes and angles, tipped by the moonlight, suggested flaring cheekbones and chiselled male beauty.

At twenty-nine, she knew enough of the score about gorgeous men. Too gorgeous, she thought, noting his brilliant dark eyes and the flash of his white teeth. Too spoilt. Lethal.

Sam drank her in from head to toe. She was nearly tall enough to reach his shoulder. He couldn't determine the exact colour of her bright waterfall of hair, but with its lustrous sheen every slight movement of her head was an invitation to touch.

His eyes had accustomed to the light now, and he could see her more clearly. It was as if the moon had picked up the shimmer in the dress and somehow transferred it to her white, pearlescent skin. The slinky, ankle-length satin seemed moulded to her, revealing with her movements the supple slenderness of her waist, sweetly rounded hips and long slim thighs. The dress's bodice was supported by a silver chain that hung from her neck. Though she kept her hands folded at her breasts, it was easy to guess at their ripe, tip-tilted lusciousness. He tried not to stare, but it was an effort to drag his eyes from her bare satin shoulders and the creamy swells just visible beneath her sheltering hands.

He was overwhelmed by such perfect female beauty; his blood stirred, and a huskiness deepened his voice. 'Isn't your boyfriend concerned about leaving you alone out here?'

She drew a sharp, quivering breath. 'But I'm not alone, am I? Though I would be if I could be. If you hadn't *insisted* on intruding on my privacy.'

'Oh. Oh, I am sorry,' he said at once, turning half away. He felt a twinge of guilt, almost as if he'd stumbled onto sacred ground. 'I'll go away.' As he turned his back he threw over his shoulder, 'Enjoy the night air.'

He took a few easy strides in the direction he'd come, but with every step away the vision lured him back with a siren's power.

'Look…Wait—just a moment, will you?'

At the sound of her sweet, low voice a pleasurable sensation he'd almost forgotten could exist shot through him. He paused, and half turned in her direction. With a casual hitch of his shoulder he said, 'Are you sure? I don't want to cause you trouble with your boyfriend.'

'Oh, don't worry about him,' she said hastily. 'He isn't… He won't cause any… Did you happen to see anyone in there dressed as Scarlett O'Hara?'

He sauntered back, as cool as if the thrill weren't gathering in his blood like a wave. 'I'm not sure I know what Scarlett O'Hara looks like.'

In an excited burst of realisation, he didn't believe the boyfriend was coming back. What man would leave this beauty out here to be accosted by strangers?

He longed to see her face, but the mask frustrated him. From what he could make out, her lips looked soft and kissable, curling up with an enticing sensitivity, as if they'd respond to the lightest tongue-flick. Her chin was delicate, with a piquancy he was sure would apply to the whole of her face.

'My moonlight fantasy,' he exclaimed with a low laugh. 'At last I've found you.'

Her eyes glittered at him through the mask, and his hand twitched with the desire to tear it away. He reached for it, but she backed away and, as though unable to free her hand from her bodice, used her elbow to gesture.

He frowned. 'Is there something wrong with your dress?' He leaned forward, his eyes narrowed for a closer look, and she stepped sharply away from him.

With the purest amusement he realised that she was holding the bodice and chain together with her hand. 'Oh, no!' he said. 'Has there been an accident? I think I can see why you're in hiding.' Instinctive thoughts of seduction crept in to colour his voice, and he added softly, 'I do hope you're wearing something under that.'

There was a tense silence. It dawned on him at last that she was embarrassed.

She surveyed him from behind her mask with glittering

eyes. 'Laugh by all means.' Her lips curved in a proud smile.
'I've no doubt this does seem very amusing to one of the *heartless* species.' Despite her brave front, some strong emotion caught at her voice, and he felt chastised.

'I'm sorry,' he said with velvet remorse. 'You're right. It's no laughing matter. But can't something be done to fix it? Some pins or something?'

She was silent for a moment, as though struggling with herself to trust his good intentions.

After a while she said stiffly, 'I tried that, but it's no good. The taffeta has started to fray now.' She eyed him through her mask for a second, then indicated one side of the bodice. 'This here is only hanging by a few threads. It was these stupid wings that did it. Whoever designed the costume—! They're far too heavy for the fabric. They were supposed to hook into the clasp at the neck, here, and here. Look…'

She half turned to give him a rear view. The dress was charmingly draped across her lower back, and as she twisted to indicate the mid-point where the wings had hooked and further damaged the fabric her hair swished a little aside to reveal an alluring glimpse of smooth white back.

His mouth dried. He imagined seeking out the ridge of her spine, tracing the bumps with his fingers, grazing all the little hollows with his lips, tasting her white satin flesh…

'We pinned this back seam as well as we could where the hook was, but it's still unravelling, and the halter chain has started to separate from the bodice.' She straightened to face him, sighing, 'It's only a matter of time before the whole thing falls apart.' After a moment she added, 'One of my girlfriends is going home to get some clothes for me.'

He supposed he deserved to have been called heartless. The woman was in an embarrassing situation, yet all his thoughts had been about caressing her. Kissing her.

The breeze picked up, teasing the hair on her neck. She gave a little shiver, and at once his imagination flew him to a parallel universe, one where he could take her with him across to that moonlit beach, lay her down beside him on the cool sand, and…

But she was cold. 'Here,' he said, and in a swift fluid movement slipped off his jacket and stepped close enough to wrap it around her shoulders.

'Oh!' She received it with a surprised jerk of her head, and the sweet summery scent of raspberries rose to his nostrils in an intoxicating cloud. 'Thanks,' she said in a soft, appealing voice that wound its way into his bloodstream like an aphrodisiac. 'Thank you very much. I really didn't expect— You're very kind.'

To his regret she drew the lapels together across her breasts, though she still held onto her bodice. The jacket swam on her feminine form, and his loins stirred at the sight.

He had to rescue her from this, he thought with urgency. Take her somewhere safe. And private. 'You can't stay out here all night,' he said. 'Why don't I take you home?'

Ellie heard the warmth in his deep voice and her sexual antennae zinged as from a high-voltage charge. This charming devil, with his smiling assurance and desire in his dark eyes, had more than rescue on his mind. As if she'd let herself be picked up! Although, in his shirtsleeves, with the power of his lean, well-made frame clearly defined, he was frankly gorgeous. And he seemed civilised, sophisticated…

When was the last time a high-powered man like him had come her way? He was a far cry from a geography teacher with the mountaineering bug.

She could see no wedding ring, though that didn't make him eligible. Hadn't she learned the hard way? The world was full of heartbreakingly attractive men who had no intention of settling down and raising families. Why else were women forced to go it alone? But—there was kindness in him. He *had* sacrificed his jacket.

His dark, sensual gaze drew hers and heat shivered through her. Unable to keep her consciousness of the pinging vibrations from her voice while she argued the pros and cons with herself, she said, 'Charmaine—I mean, Scarlett—should be back soon.'

He lifted his eyebrows. 'How long have you been waiting?'

'An hour. Maybe two.' She smiled and gave a shrug to cover her growing sense of dilemma. 'It's not my night.'

'It's not over yet.' Through the dark lashes his eyes lit with a sinful gleam, and her insides plunged into chaos. 'Come, fantasy girl. I'll take you home.'

She hesitated. 'I shouldn't really go home. I'm supposed to be in there helping to co-ordinate the programme.' And meeting Samos someone, the old Greek tycoon who was the bank's last chance. 'Are you—are you with the bank?'

'No.' His dark eyes ran over her, and she felt her flesh thrill like the breeze whispering in her hair. 'Maybe you can find some clothes here. Are any of your friends staying in the hotel overnight?'

'No. That's only for the big cheeses so they don't have to drive home afterwards.'

His brows snapped together, as though he didn't approve of that, then he gave a shrug and stood thinking.

'I'd—I'd better give you back this.' With reluctance she started to take off the jacket, but he held up his hand.

'No, no. Keep it.' His sensuous mouth edged up at the corners in a smile. 'I have a suggestion. To save you waiting for Charmaine, what if I ask the hotel to find you something to wear? You can change in my room.' He held out his hand, persuasion in his voice, smiling seduction in his eyes. 'What do you think? All right?'

This was it, she thought, her heart skipping. Just because she'd given up falling in love didn't mean she had to become a nun. It was a long time since she'd been held in a man's arms. She fingered the jacket's luxurious fabric, and inhaled its faint scent of expensive, sophisticated *man*.

He angled away slightly, as if he might walk off and leave

her, while she struggled to make up her mind to do something daring for once.

He cast her back a deep, gleaming glance beneath his lashes. It was quietly, intimately sexual, a look between adults. Man to woman, it stirred her to her feminine soul. What mature, twenty-nine-year-old career woman in charge of her life would hesitate?

'All right,' she breathed.

She allowed him to usher her through the doors, conscious of every touch, his wrist brushing hers, his hand light on her back. And for once she was lucky. There was a lift waiting, and none of the stragglers spilling from the ballroom even glanced her way.

In the light of the lift he looked to be in his late thirties. Blue highlights danced off his pitch-black hair, and there was a sardonic lilt to his black eyebrows that gave him a devilish look. Below his cheekbones, a shadow underlay his bronzed cheeks and jaw. He was a Greek god made flesh. She met the naked sensuality in his midnight eyes, and her blood surged.

'Are you staying here long?' she said, trying to keep her voice from betraying her.

He shook his head. 'I suppose you'd say I'm a guest of your bank. I hadn't intended to use the suite, but as it happens…I now have a reason.' A smile illuminated his face and shimmered in his dark eyes. 'I'm Sam.' He held out his hand.

When her ravished insides had settled back into place, the name filtered through.

Sam. An unusual name for a Greek Australian. Then re-alisation hit her. Not *that* Sam! As in Samos Stilakos. But of course it had to be. How many rich Greeks would be visiting this hotel on this night of nights?

She put her hand into his strong, warm grip, and as their palms met skin cells all along her forearm shivered with electric pleasure. 'Lovely—lovely to meet you.'

He didn't try to keep hold of her hand, as some men would have, though her flesh yearned for it. He just waited for her to respond, his eyebrows raised. The lift stopped and the doors opened before she could muster a reply.

Her brain whirred rapidly. Samos Stilakos's awesome reputation had dominated gossip in the staff canteen for the past six weeks—his daunting standards, his uncompromising stance on ethics. According to the grapevine, he'd struck terror into the department heads. She felt an extreme reluctance to tell him her name. He might end up being the big boss of the entire bank.

In the corridor she gave a light, embarrassed laugh. 'I'd rather not tell you my name, if you don't mind.'

He frowned a little, his eyes glinting.

With a pounding heart she realised he probably thought she did this sort of thing all the time. Went to hotel rooms with perfect strangers. But then, how often did *he* do it? Quite often, judging by how smoothly this little operation had gone. How would it go down for her future in the bank, if she knew he seduced vulnerable employees?

For her job's sake she should leave now. Thrust the jacket back at him, ignore the risks, and risk walking out to the taxi rank. At least she'd have the mask.

She should. But she let him guide her down the hall to Room 525, and, with her adrenaline flowing, watched his smooth, olive-tanned fingers slide in the key.

The room was pleasantly furnished in the impersonal style of hotel rooms. The counterpane on the king-sized bed had been turned down, and lamps on either side cast a soft apricot glow.

The door closed behind her and she turned to face him. The room sprang alive with sexual possibilities.

He nodded to her, 'Make yourself comfortable.' He strolled to the desk and picked up the phone, murmured a few words into it, then covered the receiver. 'How does a maid's uniform sound?' She nodded and he spoke again, appraising her, his black lashes half lowered over his dark, sensual gaze. 'About five-seven. Size ten. Thank you.'

He strolled back to her with an easy, hospitable smile. 'It will take a few minutes. Would you like a drink after your ordeal?' He made a lazy gesture towards the mini-bar.

'No. No, thanks.' She tried to sound casual, to match his relaxed demeanour, but her senses were in uproar.

He said abruptly, 'Would you feel better if I went away?'

He was giving her an option, she realised, relieved her instincts about his essential decency had been right. She raised her chin. 'No, don't. Don't go.' Despite her bravado her voice sounded croaky, as if it was about to dry up.

Samos Stilakos didn't look ill at ease, however. He pulled off his tie and tossed it to a chair, the shimmer back in his dark eyes. 'Won't you take off your mask?'

'I'd rather not,' she said with a careless smile, knowing how rude and ungrateful and insanely weird it sounded, after he'd so kindly rescued her. 'Not yet.'

He moved closer, his gaze warm and compelling, and said softly, 'But I think I'll feel uncomfortable kissing a woman without knowing her eyes and face.'

She closed her eyes. The blood was thundering in her ears. 'Who—who said anything about kissing?'

Almost lazily he reached out to curve his lean, smooth fingers under her chin, tilted up her face, and bent to brush her mouth with his.

At the first touch, excitement ignited in her blood. He drew away, leaving her breathless, fire dancing along her lips. He frowned down at her, a flame in the depths of his eyes, then drew her firmly against his hard body, and kissed her properly, while her breasts swelled and her lips parted.

With sensual artistry he took first her upper lip, then the lower lip between his, to tease and tantalise until her knees gave way. Then he captured both lips firmly, and slipped his tongue inside her mouth, inflaming the delicate tissues while her bones liquefied and she nearly swooned.

Wildfire rose in her blood.

It was nothing, nothing like she'd ever experienced. So tender, so wildly, thrillingly arousing. It was as if he knew how to kiss a woman as a woman dreamed of being kissed.

A raw sound came from her throat, and she thrust her soft curves into the lean angles of his muscular frame. Forgetting her fragile dress, she linked her arms around his neck and clutched at his hair, aware with excitement of his big, vibrant body's charged response to her. Eagerly she helped him push the jacket from her shoulders, and let it slide.

He deepened the sizzling intensity of the kiss. In some way liberated by the mask, she threw aside constraint, and, instead of her usual polite co-operation, matched him tongue for tongue, caress for caress, without inhibition.

She was hardly aware that the weak threads of her satin bodice had given way, removing one of the barriers between his iron-hard body and her sensitised skin. Grazed by the friction of his clothes and belt buckle, her bare nipples thrilled to the delicious contact.

She'd never experienced such instant desire. Hotly aroused, she felt one of his seductive hands close over her breast, while the other slid to her nape, trailed tinglingly over her scalp, then snaked through her hair to pluck at the string of her mask.

At once her survivor instinct clicked in. In a lightning reflex, her hands shot up to secure the mask, and she broke from him. 'No,' she panted hoarsely. 'Don't take it off.'

He stared back, fire in his eyes as they devoured her naked breasts. His voice was rough and gravelly. 'Why not? Why does it matter? Are you married?'

'No. I just don't want you to see my face.'

'Why not? I need to know who you are.' He gestured with his hands. 'Don't get me wrong. It's erotic making love to a mystery woman, in a kinky sort of way. I might even get a taste for it. But if you stay with me tonight…'

His voice thickened with the words, and she sensed how much he wanted it. Wanted *her*. Somehow, it strengthened her instinct to keep her face covered. She said in a low, firm voice, 'I won't stay unless I can leave the mask on.'

He stared at her. 'You're not serious.'

'I am serious. I am.'

Calculation glimmered in his eyes, as if he was recognising the real possibility of his moonlit fantasy slipping away from him, then his lashes lowered.

'Try to see it my way.' His deep voice was almost a purr. He held out his hands and advanced to back her gently against the wall, his long muscular thighs grazing hers, melting her with his devastating sexual power. 'I don't want to feel I'm taking advantage of you.' With one long, tanned finger he trailed fire down her throat to the valley between her breasts, fanning her sweet erotic craving, and she burned for him to go further.

'Love-making shouldn't be an impersonal thing,' he said persuasively. 'If I can't see into your eyes it feels—soulless. Can't you understand?'

He was so meltingly, mouth-wateringly sexy, so honourable, she wavered. But just as his mouth began to tease her ear, turning her veins to liquid fire, some cool little internal voice piped up to remind her that the last time she'd believed a man was honourable she'd given him two years of her life, and he'd left her without a word.

His lips blazed a scorching trail down her throat and she shuddered with pleasure. 'I do see, and I do want to stay,' she panted when she could speak, 'but only if you agree not to snatch the mask off. And not—not to ask me my name.'

'But how will I find you again if I don't know your name?'

Even in her state of arousal she knew the smooth words for a ploy. 'You won't want to.' Wry cynicism deepened her huskiness. 'And I won't want you to.'

He drew back, a frown in his eyes. 'But you want me. You can't deny it.'

'Yes, yes. I admit it.' She leaned back against the wall and sighed, and stretched her arms voluptuously over her head, unable to keep her hungry gaze from his shirt-opening with its dark, sultry promise of chest hair. 'I do want you,' she said with throaty conviction, imagining the salt taste of that bronzed, hair-roughened skin. 'But only tonight.'

He gave a sexy, disbelieving laugh. 'Isn't that my line?' Then his brows drew together and he stared at her in bemusement. She could see how used he was to women falling at his feet. He took a deep breath, reefed his hand through his black hair. 'Why do you say that? Why only tonight?'

An amused, sophisticated little smile played about his mouth, but she could tell he was piqued. She supposed with his assets it was natural. She could hardly explain that, since the end of her romantic dreams, her job security was of critical importance. She wasn't one of those women who could face down gossip about their sexual antics with the bosses. If he took over the bank and news of this got out, she'd have to leave, if he didn't sack her first.

She touched his hand. 'You're very attractive, but I don't want an affair. Affairs use a woman up. If I stay with you tonight it will only be this one time, and you'll have to agree not to take off my mask.'

He shook his head. 'If I see you again,' he said, his tone charming but insistent, 'I'll know you, with or without the mask. I'd know the shape of you and the way you hold your head. Your mouth…' His voice deepened. The flame smouldered in his dark eyes, and she was tempted, *how* she was tempted, to wrap herself around his hard body. 'And that red hair is—unforgettable.'

'It's strawberry,' she corrected huskily. But she could see his point. He might recognise her again. If she stayed with him, she had little choice but to appeal to his gentlemanly instincts not to blab about her all over the building. And she wanted to stay, she realised, with an upsurge of desire.

'All right.' She could almost see the flat nipples under his shirt, and wantonness dripped from her voice like honey. 'If I ever did meet you again, and you recognised me, you would have to promise that you'd never, ever refer to what happens between us this night. To anyone.'

He gave a sharp, disbelieving laugh. 'As if I would—' He took a couple of impatient strides away and flung out his arms. 'Why should I? I don't bargain, and I don't make promises to get a woman into my bed.' He paused, his shoulders tense, and said with a cool shrug, 'The only promise I can make to you, sweetheart, is the one of giving you pleasure. If that isn't enough, we'd better both forget it.' He smiled, but there was an edge to his voice, his dark eyes glinting, his face suddenly proud and unrelenting, like the uncompromising Samos Stilakos she'd heard so much about.

It made him even more wildly desirable, if possible, and when the rejection had sunk in her disappointment was potent, but she said with dignity, 'Then I'll leave.'

He looked incredulous, and was about to speak when there was a discreet knock.

He tucked in his shirt and went to open the door. After a few murmured words he came back with a package, and thrust it to her with a burning, sardonic look. 'Your dress.'

She accepted it, her hands trembling, and with a muttered 'thank you' took it into the bathroom.

The maid's uniform was a white zip-up dress. She dragged off the ruined costume and threw it in the bin. Goodbye fantasy woman, she grimaced as she zipped the uniform. It was tightish, and only covered her to mid-thigh. But at least it was decent.

She raised the mask for a glimpse of her face, and met a stranger in the mirror. Her mouth was swollen from kissing, her blue eyes heavy-lidded, languorous with unfulfilled passion. Like his beautiful, expressive eyes. If only…

Images of the pleasures she'd turned down rose to torment her. She'd never met anyone like him before, or experienced such chemistry. But it was too late now, she reflected regretfully. She'd insulted him, and now he could hardly wait to get rid of her. She braced herself, and, with the mask back in place, opened the door.

Samos Stilakos stood waiting, brooding tension in the set of his powerful shoulders, his thick black lashes downcast. He looked ready to leave, his jacket slung over his shoulder. He'd rolled his sleeves back a little, and she could see the dusky hairs curling on his bronzed, sinewy forearms.

He looked up. His dark eyes riveted to her, intent and smoulderingly sexual.

Her blood started to boom in her ears with a heavy, sensual beat.

'Come here,' he said thickly.

The fierce fire in his eyes compelled her. She felt a burning, primeval urgency to run into his arms and press her lips to his throat, but some stronger part of her forced her to her resolve and clamped her feet to the floor. 'Only if you promise…'

She held her breath.

The deep voice, when it came, was harsh. 'I promise.'

She allowed herself to advance a step, desire torching through her like a fever. Dared she risk pushing him further? She breathed, 'And do you agree, even if we should meet again, never to refer to this night, or to anything that happens between us here?'

The silence simmered while his dark, molten eyes raked her from head to toe. Her yearning for him reached a torrid pitch. She imagined his hard, virile length thrusting and thrusting to fill her. The sublime, delicious pleasure…

His mouth quivered. 'I agree,' he said rawly, then threw away his jacket, and in one long stride covered the distance between them and pulled her into his arms.

CHAPTER ONE

FOUR months later, Ellie sat at her desk, settling into the pre-carious role as latest in a string of PAs to the most ruthless and exacting boss the Sirius Bank had ever known. It was twenty-six days since she'd landed the job, and how she'd done it she still wasn't sure. But there was one thing she was sure of.

Sam Stilakos had a very poor memory.

Or a seriously overcrowded sex-life. How else could he have forgotten the night that blazed in her memory like an inferno? Not that she wanted him to remember, she hastened to reflect. If he did she'd be out on her twenty-nine-year-old ear with her life's plan shot to pieces.

Even so, it was distinctly lowering for a woman to discover how completely forgettable she was.

For a while she'd wondered if he was just a very good actor, but she'd stopped thinking that now. Not once in the weeks of seeing him every day, working with him in the tense atmo-sphere of his office, meeting his deep, inscrutable gaze across the table at board meetings, melting to his dark chocolate voice on the intercom—and he buzzed her constantly for the most finicky reasons—had he shown the merest flicker of recogni-tion. Or flirtatiousness. Just scrupulous politeness.

No wonder his ex-wife had issues with him.

A crash from inside his office jolted Ellie from her reverie. The wife's visit wasn't going well. At almost the same moment she glanced around to see an elegantly groomed older lady appear at the outer door. The woman approached the desk, and, with the assured charm of her years, introduced herself as Irene Stilakos.

Ellie concealed her intense fascination behind her professional face. So this was Sam's mother. But she wasn't Greek!

'He's had an unexpected visitor.' Ellie smiled up into shrewd grey eyes, wondering if Irene had heard the crash. 'He shouldn't be long. Would you like a coffee while you wait?' She indicated the plush armchairs in the small lounge area by the window.

Irene Stilakos smiled a refusal, and selected a chair. Behind her, Sydney glittered in the morning sun like a jewel, but oblivious to the scene, she bypassed the pile of recent glossies and picked up a copy of Sirius's annual report.

She looks friendly, Ellie thought, covertly searching for a resemblance to Sam's stunning chiselled features and imperious dark eyes. With her softly waved hair and lively, pleasant face, you'd never believe she had a son so—

The door to Sam's inner office burst open. Ellie jumped, and Sam's mother looked up as a shrill, impassioned voice rent the air. 'Anyone can make a mistake, Sam! Haven't you ever heard the concept of forgiveness?'

There was a deep, curt response, then the pert rear view of Natalie, television soap star and Sam's ex-wife, appeared in the doorway, arms flailing. 'You know why you're scared to come to my wedding, lover?' she screeched. 'Because you haven't been able to find another woman in four years. And do you know why that is, Sam? Do you know why? I'll tell you why. Because you can't replace *me*! And you never—ever—*will*.'

She slammed the door so hard Ellie's filing cabinet shuddered. Then midway in storming across the room she halted, muttering, to feverishly rifle her bag.

She wore impossibly high heels Ellie had no trouble in identifying as Jimmy Choos, and a minuscule leather dress with peep-holes that showed her fabulous all-over tan. A flick of her ragged blonde designer hair, with its fashionable black roots, revealed the obligatory tattoo on her shoulder.

She looked like trouble. *Sexy* trouble, exactly the sort men went mad for.

Unconsciously Ellie patted the smooth coil at her nape. No wonder she'd made no lasting impression. She'd considered going completely blonde herself when Sam had taken over as boss, but had gone the other way instead, choosing a deep, rich, camouflaging red. It seemed to have worked well. Too well, she sometimes thought.

She watched as Natalie pulled out a handful of tissues to dab at her professionally modelled nose. All at once the blonde's eye fell on Sam's mother, and she froze rigid.

Her fashionable pout grew puffier and more defensive. 'Well?'

Irene Stilakos started, and sat straighter in her chair. 'Oh,' she said hurriedly. 'Don't mind me, Natalie. I was just thinking you should be careful in those heels. You need to look after those bones in your lower spine. Think ahead, dear, to when you'll be bearing children.'

Natalie hissed in an outraged breath, then to Ellie's alarm she whipped around to her. 'And what are you staring at, Miss Mouse? Hoping you might have a chance with him? It's what you've been hanging out for, isn't it?'

Ellie felt her face flame scarlet. Her lips parted in stunned denial, but there was no silencing her accuser.

'Don't try to deny it.' Natalie's rather high-pitched voice vibrated with passion. 'I've heard you talk to him in that drooly-drooly voice. You're after him. You all are. Don't you think a woman knows?'

Ellie scrabbled for her professional poise and drew herself up, searingly conscious of Sam's *mother* sitting there. And Sam himself was very sharp of hearing. 'That may just be the way I talk,' she retorted as coolly as humanly possible, in her low, admittedly quite husky voice. 'I don't have the luxury of screaming or throwing things. And I have too much work to do to go after anyone.'

'Yeah, right.' Natalie's brittle laugh rang out in the quiet room. 'Just look at her, will you? It's written all over her face.' She shrugged and started for the exit. 'You're welcome to the cold-blooded brute, if you think you can measure up to him.' Her eyes filled up with tears. 'Try living with a perfectionist.' Out in the corridor she flung rawly over her shoulder, 'See what's it like to be dispensable.' With a despairing hair-flick she stalked off in the direction of the lifts.

Ellie gathered her shell-shocked self together to find Sam's mother piercing her with her penetrating grey gaze, intensified by the lenses of her glasses.

'It isn't true,' Ellie said quickly. 'I don't like him at all.' Then, recollecting who she was talking to, she rushed to add, 'I mean—he's very good-looking, and brilliant and everything, but he's not at all my type. He's far too demanding, and arrogant, and bossy. Not that that's a bad thing, of course, when he's the boss.' She made a weak attempt at a laugh. 'Please don't be offended—'

Sam's mother gave her a worried smile, as if she needed convincing.

'—but I actually prefer less high-powered men. You know— friendlier.' Her recurring vision of herself enfolded in Sam's strong arms, his stirringly sexy mouth, his midnight satin eyes slumbrous with desire, swam into her mind, but she forced herself to stay on course. 'I like men who are more—accessible. Emotionally. Do you know what I mean?'

This was, in fact, a bare-faced lie. She only ever fell madly in love with inappropriate men who were totally *in*accessible.

Sam's mother seemed to know it, because she frowned at Ellie and gave her head a very slight shake. Ellie thought she must have gone too far and had better backtrack, and lowered her voice confidentially. 'I don't mean he isn't good to work for. He is, he's wonderful, and he can be so-o-o charming to people who don't irritate him, but in a personal, or—or *sexual* sense I could never find him attractive at—'

She broke off. Sam's mother's gaze had shifted to a point somewhere above and to the right of Ellie, and Ellie had a horrible sinking feeling that someone was standing at Sam's door. She glanced down and saw a pair of handmade leather shoes, polished to a very high gloss, trouser legs of the finest fabric, and knew immediately who.

Her dismayed gaze travelled the lean, powerful length of Samos Stilakos, and connected with his intelligent dark eyes, brimming with an expression she couldn't quite read. There was a sardonic quirk to his sensuous mouth, and his black eyebrows were drawn.

Her heart jarred to a halt.

'Come in,' he said, holding the door wide for Irene without taking his eyes from Ellie. Irene gave her a warm glance as she went past, and Sam said in deep, clipped tones, 'I'll talk to you later, Eleanor.'

He closed the door.

Ellie plunged into turmoil. How long had he been standing there? She covered her burning cheeks. There was no chance he hadn't heard some of it.

What if Irene told Sam of Natalie's accusation? Wasn't it only natural she would? She would. Of course she would. She'd be telling him even now.

Sam absently steered his mother through some scattered shards of antique vase and across the luxurious expanse of his office. While she settled herself on the deep red leather chesterfield, he wandered over to stare moodily at the view from his wall-sized window. Curious how a couple of smudgy little clouds could take the shine off Sydney Harbour. That bridge could look bloody grim.

'She seems like a lovely girl, Sam,' his mother commented, crossing her ankles.

Sam gave a shrug, but something like a skewer slid through his intestines. *Why* had she said she didn't like him? Could he have offended her in some way?

He scrolled back through their exchanges about work. Her mouth was often grave—intriguingly so, for a woman whose blue eyes could actually glitter at times with mischief—but she'd seemed happy enough, calm and competent. She'd coped with all the projects he'd thrust her into with cool efficiency, surprising him at times with her instinctive grasp of the big picture.

She was a little too inclined to try injecting her feminine viewpoint into his careful strategies for the bank's recovery, but he could easily keep that under control. In all other ways he still found her—pleasing.

He'd honoured his agreement with her, and would continue to do so, although it had been extracted under duress. Her total rejection of an affair was impressive. Although…what more tantalising challenge had ever been given a man?

Not that he condoned personal relationships in the workplace. Purists might argue that he shouldn't have placed her so close to him. It had been a business decision, no more, no less, to keep his eye on her. In fact, once or twice he had actually fantasised having a section of the wall removed so he could see her face.

That face. For an instant his eyes drifted shut. The curious breathless feeling he experienced whenever she entered the room came over him. It was amazing how, once a woman's face had been forbidden to a man, that face could become so infinitely more alluring and desirable than any other.

But… He knew the rules and there was no risk. That invisible line she'd drawn around herself was as definite as a castle moat, and in twenty-six days he'd never tried to cross it. Not once.

So if she was unhappy… He felt a skidding sensation inside his chest. Could it be something to do with *that night*?

His mother cut in on his thoughts. She was studying him with a thoughtful gaze, her head a little on one side. 'I don't think you should take the things she said personally, dear. She assured me she only meant it in the sexual sense.'

He gave a careless laugh. 'Is that what she said?' Nevertheless the skewer made a savage twist. Women *always* found him attractive in the sexual sense. If Eleanor O'Dea was the woman he thought she was, whom his instincts told him she must be, she had every reason to find him sexually attractive.

Unless…unless he was mistaken.

He thought back to the first time he'd laid eyes on her after he'd taken on the bank. Wasn't it the Christmas party—?

He frowned, recalling how once again he'd been taken aback by the scale of it. Mature men and women carousing, hugging each other in boozy camaraderie at the company's expense, some far-gone woman from Sales actually performing a dreamy, inebriated dance on a table-top. When he'd enquired as to who had been responsible for organising this latest orgiastic extravaganza, someone had pointed out Ellie.

The name.

His lungs had momentarily seized, for there she'd been, a tallish slender woman standing quietly in the middle of the scene of riotous debauchery, in the thick of it, but in some strange way alone, as if she occupied her own small pool of serenity.

It was *her*, he was certain. Straight away he'd noticed her soft, curly lips. And her skin. How incredibly pure and satin-white he'd remembered it being, in contrast with her bright hair, and looked to be still under the revolving strobe light. But it was seeing her eyes for the first time that had affected him most. Luminous, sapphire eyes, with long curled lashes, sparkling at the antics of her colleagues like some laughing female devil's.

She'd been wearing very high heels and some brown thing— or was it beige?—with what looked like a strange glitch in its neckline. As he recalled, it had been quite shapeless. In fact most of the things she wore failed to make the most of her shape. The moonlit shape that haunted him.

His frown deepened. He hadn't been able to take his eyes off her, but when she'd glanced across at him, unbelievably those lovely eyes had looked straight through him.

It had shaken him. Could he have been mistaken?

His mother hastened to soothe him. 'It's not that she doesn't like you for yourself, dear, I'm sure. I think she's exactly what you need out there.' She gazed earnestly at him and added, her eyes as innocent as the dawn, 'Natalie didn't like her one bit.'

Natalie. A grenade lodged in his vitals, but he didn't move a muscle. 'Didn't she?' he said without expression. 'When did Natalie ever like another woman?'

'That's true,' Irene conceded, sending him a quick, searching glance. 'Natalie can be very threatened by the sort of woman she can't compete with.' She clasped her hands. 'That was what I wanted to talk to you about.'

Sam saw the anxiety in his mother's face, and shelved the mystery of his enigmatic PA. A woman who could so easily dismiss the most torrid sex he'd ever experienced was either an actress or a fool. And why a woman so lusciously endowed with feminine charms felt no need to display them to advantage was frustrating, but hardly important. As for her claiming not to *like* him— From what he could gather, Ellie O'Dea was one of the more popular staff members. She seemed to like everyone else, so why not him? As he recalled, she'd certainly liked him on that night.

'Sam?'

He snapped into focus. 'All right.' He dropped into the chair facing her. 'Go on, then.' Resignedly, he raised a hand to motion her on. 'Let's hear it—the wedding.'

Irene sat on the sofa's edge, the better to make her pitch. Her son's face was patient, but wary, his dark eyes watchful beneath their black lashes. She would have to tread carefully. After Natalie and the divorce she'd seen a tougher layer of cynicism added to his sophistication. His resemblance to his proud father ran deeper than his Greek colouring and hard male beauty. His handsome, urbane surface concealed a well of feelings that wouldn't easily be touched a second time.

'I'll be honest with you, Sam,' she began. 'I'm a little nervous about going to the wedding on my own. My being there is bound to upset Natalie, and she's such a volatile girl, who knows what might happen?' Her hand stole to her heart.

Sam noted the unconscious gesture with a frown.

'If your father were still alive—'

He leaned forward and took her lined hands in his strong, smooth ones. 'If Papa were alive he wouldn't let you go.' He made the effort to gentle his voice. 'You don't have to, you know. You could decline.'

'And then this horrible feud would go on! No, dear, whatever your father would have thought, I can't be cut off from my family for the rest of my life. For all his faults I miss my brother, and, although you'll never admit it to yourself, you must miss Michael. He's not only your cousin, he's still the closest friend you ever had.'

A blistering retort rose to Sam's lips but he suppressed it. Her frail heart wasn't up to the savage passions generated by the betrayal of his honour. It was clear enough what she was about to ask for. His attendance at his cousin's wedding.

To his ex-wife.

Smooth it all over, as though it had never happened. His fractured life patched together under a coat of gloss.

It had been a while, he mused, since he'd wanted to cut out both their hearts. Now he only wanted to wipe them from the universe, but he'd never mention it to Irene. She was a woman—essentially not even Greek. His father would have understood, if the strain of the dishonour hadn't killed him.

'I won't go to their wedding.' The intensity of the quiet words resonated in the silence for seconds.

His mother nodded. 'No one could blame you, Sam, but if you don't go, this myth Natalie's spreading around—that you can't get over her—will seem to be confirmed. Even my brother seems convinced you can't look at another woman.' She rolled her eyes. 'He wrote me such a sympathetic note, asking about your state of mind. "If Sam doesn't want to come we'll understand," he said. "Has poor Sam made any progress?" I have to admit, dear, I found it quite galling.'

Sam broke into a sardonic laugh. Though it was true he hadn't looked for a replacement. There'd been no woman in his life since the divorce. Perhaps lately his apartment had begun to seem quiet, tomb-like even, but one Natalie was enough for a lifetime. In the beginning he'd thought their differences would soon be ironed out, but they had only seemed to widen with time. There'd been no meeting of minds, no shared humour. The charmingly volatile young woman he'd married was too often a spoilt, destructive child. Too much of a child herself to be prepared for the responsibilities of parenthood.

His gut clenched at the memory of the unforgivable thing she'd done in the name of her career. Eventually she'd dragged his cousin into an affair, scandalised his family, and ended by splitting it in halves.

It occurred to him then, as he listened to his mother discussing the arrangements for Natalie's next wedding, that if he ever sought another woman she would be different. More subtle and elusive. The sort of woman who could inspire a man's imagination.

As it often had since the night of the masked ball, a vision surfaced in his mind. And the more he saw of Ellie O'Dea, the more he listened to her low, husky voice on the intercom— sometimes he called her just to make her talk—the more he was convinced that his first overwhelming instinct about her had been correct.

She was the fantasy woman. At least, he thought so. Since acquiring the bank, he'd examined several possible candidates, but it was amazing how many tallish, slim, red-haired women there were working in the building. Though none of the others had had her curious power of dislocating his lungs, he wanted to be absolutely sure. What he really needed was to see more of that fascinating arrangement of curves.

If only he could see her in different clothes, outside the office context. Perhaps he could arrange a conference, or a business dinner where she'd be obliged to wear something more revealing. Clinging, even. Satin.

And he was damned if he wouldn't break down that barrier of reserve. The very idea of her not finding him attractive was laughable. He could enjoy watching her eat those words. In fact, it wasn't too much of a stretch to say that she'd flung him the challenge all over again.

At the possibilities this conjured his red blood cells stirred to the music and sprang to the salute. Dammit, if he couldn't find a way to rediscover the awe-inspiring flexibility of that slim, willowy body his name wasn't Sam Stilakos!

But...

He drummed his fingers morosely on the chair arms. The promise. It always came back to that bloody promise. Whilever he was bound by that ridiculous verbal contract he could see no way forward. With her gloriously passionate nature so cunningly hidden beneath her demure office persona, she was as maddeningly distant from him as some mediaeval princess in an ivory tower. Unless she could somehow be encouraged to break the embargo herself...

His mother's voice, still on about weddings and grandchildren, finally filtered through. 'I don't know why you can't find a nice girl, Sam. It's a pity you're so choosy.'

He stirred himself to reach over to his desk for his diary. 'It is,' he agreed, flipping it open to the day's schedule.

'If you could only find some lovely girl to take, it would shut them all up. I'd love to wipe the smug grins off their faces.' She heaved a sigh. 'If only I had a daughter to go with. Some nice, sensible girl I could rely on. Don't you have anyone here you could ask?' Her eyes flitted over his face, and beyond him to the view. She clutched at her heart and said, a brave little quaver in her voice, 'I suppose I'll just have to go it alone, and hope I don't drop dead in a strange place.' Dejectedly, she dragged herself to her feet.

Sam got up with her and gave her a bracing hug. 'Don't worry. I'm sure they have medical facilities in Queensland.'

Despite her talent as an actress, he knew her anxiety was well-founded. Natalie could be a hellcat, and the wedding would be stressful, not a good situation for Irene's health. Wild horses wouldn't get him there, but if she had to go it was up to him to find a means to protect her. Perhaps, he mused, he could send someone to support her in his absence.

It would take some calm, sensible person. Someone with exceptional interpersonal skills. Preferably someone who could stand parties.

An inspiration seized him then that was so fantastically brilliant, such sheer, diabolical genius, he was nearly swept away. Someone—*someone*—who'd need the appropriate clothes.

Suddenly energised, he planted a kiss on his mother's soft cheek. 'Leave it with me,' he said, the old thrill rising in his veins like an elixir. 'I'll find someone to go with you.'

Ellie sat slumped in her chair. A month in the job and she was finished. She wouldn't even have lasted as long as Sasha, Sam's first PA when he'd taken over as CEO.

Her thoughts flew back to the staff Christmas party, delegated, as usual, to her. The festivities had been in full swing before Sam had finished meeting with Gary, the finance manager, and descended from his alpine heights on the fifty-fifth floor for a brief chilly drink with the staff.

She'd done her best for Gary, writing out in detail exactly what he had to say to Sam in defence of the functions budget. A pity she'd had to leave it to Gary to deliver himself.

She hadn't spotted Sam at the party straight away. She'd been far too busy negotiating with Gary to come in off the ledge, but when she *had* seen Sam she'd been rocked by the sheer physical impact of once more being in the same room as him.

In the living, breathing flesh, in a suit cut by a master's hand to celebrate his wide shoulders, narrow hips and long powerful limbs, he was even more stunning than she'd remembered, his brilliant dark eyes more stirring. But the sight of him surrounded by all the executives eager to defer to him had made her realise how inaccessible he was to the likes of her.

That was when she'd noticed Sasha, enticing him to dance. She'd been flirting with him, swishing her long burgundy hair around in an obvious attempt to captivate him.

He'd declined, but by the time Ellie had recovered from her frozen shock she'd done the only possible thing, and pretended not to know him.

Rumour had it that poor, besotted Sasha had later draped herself around Sam's neck in the corridor and attempted to seduce him. Whether or not it was true was unclear, but what *was* clear was that when the office had reopened after the Christmas break Sasha had gone. Transferred to one of the Brisbane branches, someone had said. They'd all shuddered.

After Sasha there'd been an astonishingly rapid series of PAs who hadn't lasted the first week of their probation. Occasional glimpses of them had been caught on the lower floors as Samos Stilakos strode through the departments on snap inspections. They had followed along two-steps behind, gazing at him in adoration like Sasha, or blatant lust like auburn-haired Vanessa, but as quickly as they had seemed to snaffle the job, they had disappeared.

Ellie wouldn't even have dreamed of drawing attention to herself by applying, if it hadn't been for a fateful encounter with the man himself.

It had been after the staff farewell to Prue in HR. Poor Prue, still a beauty at forty-seven, had sacrificed the possibility of motherhood in search of a long-term relationship, and had ended up missing out on both.

Ellie had gone to great lengths to make the party one of her best. Afterwards, she'd been directing the caterers' tidy-up in the dishevelled function room, when a sudden fall in the noise level had alerted her to the presence of The Boss.

Her heart had gone into a series of crazed spins as he'd paused at the entrance, all six-three of commanding masculinity, his hair so black it was nearly blue, dark, lean and sternly handsome in a well-cut navy suit, with a crisp blue shirt and purple silk tie.

Her midnight lover.

He'd cast an appraising eye over the suddenly frozen activity in the room, then strolled the entire length of it to her.

Her heart had nearly stopped. Had he recognised her?

Once more he'd captured her in his dark, mesmeric gaze. 'Ellie O'Dea, isn't it?'

Somehow, hearing her name wrapped for the first time in that deep chocolaty timbre transported her straight back to that sizzling hotel room. Or maybe it had been the faint, tantalising spiciness of his aftershave. Or the controlled self-possession of his sensual, severely sculpted mouth.

Whatever, the flame he'd ignited in her blood that night flared back to intoxicated life.

'Yes,' she admitted breathlessly, once she'd recalled it. 'It is. Eleanor.' Automatically she held out her hand. The instant he took it in his firm, warm grasp, ninety thousand volts of electricity thrilled in recognition along her arm.

Did he want to thank her for the party? Perhaps, as she'd so often fantasised, with just the hint of a twinkle in his eye?

But his deep dark eyes were merely as cool and searching as any boss's meeting a prospective employee for the first time. 'Are you ambitious, Eleanor?'

Eleanor. Now why on earth had she told him to call her that? No one had called her Eleanor since she was five. 'I am, yes,' she tried to respond with the poise appropriate to a twenty-nine-year-old career woman with supremely marketable skills. Although, to be honest, she was confused. She knew he'd promised not to refer to that night, but he could have at least smiled.

'A vacancy has arisen in Executive Management for a PA,' he said with impersonal calm. 'It will be gazetted in tomorrow's Staff Bulletin before it goes out on the net. You might consider applying for it.'

She stared at him. A *job*? she might have said if she weren't in shock, but by the time she recovered he'd already walked away, detachment in every brisk, autocratic stride. The reality slowly sank through.

He hadn't recognised her.

At home that evening she drew the tattered mask from the satin box where she kept it, along with the postcards Mark had sent from remote locations around the globe, and other romantic memorabilia. She tried it on, and studied herself in the mirror from every angle.

To be fair, it covered quite a lot of her face, and gave her nose an entirely different shape. In her suit and with her hair severely pulled back, she supposed she bore little resemblance to the woman at the ball. But shouldn't there still be something—some indefinable thing that was unique to her?

She couldn't wait to get her hands on the bulletin, and was at work even earlier than usual next morning to comb her pigeon-hole. As she'd hoped, the PA advertised for was his. His latest—experienced Schanelle with her sleek coppery bob, and, it had been wildly rumoured, references from Donald Trump—hadn't survived the week.

Someone in HR must have recommended her. Looking on the bright side, it was exciting, even flattering, to be included in the selection list out of a thousand employees. Professional recognition was something. She'd certainly done enough study over the years to give her the academic qualifications. And, despite the risk of him eventually realising who she was and despatching her to the back of beyond, the salary was strongly tempting. It would bring the goal she'd set for herself into view as a distinct possibility.

And she knew better than to follow the example of her predecessors, who hadn't been able to resist advertising their wares to him.

But underneath she was disappointed. Maybe it was irrational, but she wanted him to have guessed who she was. She'd had a sneaking little hope that he had, in fact, recognised her, but was honouring the promise she'd extracted from him by pretending not to.

The job offer wrote off that hope, though. Samos Stilakos would never allow her to work near him if he knew who she was. Unless…unless she'd meant more to him on that tumultuous night than just another one-night stand. Unless the job was a means of getting to know her!

What a laugh. There she was again, backsliding into fruitless romanticism.

'It's like being chosen by Henry the Eighth,' Beth, her friend, said, wrinkling her brow. 'Are you sure you want to risk it? What if he does eventually recognise you? God knows where you might be transferred. And what are your chances of not falling in love with him? At the Staff Appreciation Breakfast I even saw Schanelle ogling him with her mouth open.'

Ellie wondered how she could have missed that. She'd probably been occupied with settling the blood-feud that had arisen between the hired chef and the wait staff.

'If I keep my professional distance I should be safe,' she argued. 'And there's no chance I could fall in love with a man so— *spoiled* by women he can't tell one from another.' Indignation nearly got the better of her. 'Anyway. I told you. I've given up falling in love.' She noted Beth's unconvinced frown. No doubt mentally leafing back through the notorious O'Dea files.

All right, so once or twice she'd had her heart broken and her dreams shattered. It had cost her a few sleepless nights to be thrown over in favour of an ice-field, she could now freely admit. But that was the old Ellie O'Dea. She was stronger now, and in charge of her own life. Her heart was still there, large as life, but she'd locked it in an armour-plated box and it would never betray her again. If it showed any signs of weakening to the charms of some smiling predator, she had only to think of Mark.

'I have to think what the salary would mean,' she told Beth firmly. 'Samos Stilakos doesn't recognise me, it's a great job, and I need the money. End of story.'

Beth eyed Ellie's suit with the knowledgeable air securely married women used for their less fortunate friends. 'You could get some new clothes. Brand-new. Like from real shops. In fact, I think you'd have to, in that position.'

'Possibly,' Ellie allowed stiffly. 'But I'm thinking of more important things. I'm not getting any younger. With the salary hike I could reach my target a year earlier.'

'Oh,' Beth muttered. 'Right. Your target.' She straightened the flowers in the vase she kept on her desk, replenished at least twice daily by her adoring husband. 'Look, Ellie, you don't have to give up yet. You're not even thirty, for goodness' sake.'

'When should I give up? Thirty-two? Thirty-three? Or wait till thirty-six when my poor brave little ovary buckles under the strain?'

Beth knew her ovary saga, and what the doctors had warned. 'Don't waste too much time to have your children,' they'd told Ellie back in her late teens after the painful cyst had been removed. 'There's no predicting how long your egg production will continue.'

It wasn't just the damaging scar tissue that had been left behind. It was the distinct possibility that it could happen again, and ruin the other ovary's chances as well.

She hadn't thought twice about children until Isabella, her sister, had given birth to her first little girl. Ellie would never forget the day. It had been just one week after Mark had left her.

She could still see Isabella gazing radiantly at the newborn in her arms, while her awed sisters crowded around the hospital bed, exclaiming over the baby's tiny pink perfections. 'Every woman should have a daughter,' Isabella had crooned on high from her cloud.

Ellie had been stabbed then with such a sickening bolt of fear, she could still feel the pain of it. What if she'd left it too late already? What if she *never had a child*?

She had driven from the hospital with a growing certainty that she shouldn't waste any more time. Waiting and hoping for the next man to come along was a fool's game. Recent events had proven something she had long suspected. Though men might desire her, she was not a woman who could inspire a man to love her.

If she wanted a child, she'd have to go it alone. And she should do it while she still could, even if she had to break rules.

She knew Beth didn't approve. Thousands wouldn't. She could hardly bear to think of it herself when she tried to imagine herself actually going to an IVF clinic, and admitting to some professional that she was forced to resort to a clinical procedure.

It was all very well for happily married people who were secure in their egg supply. Beth thought she should rush down to David Jones and splurge her savings on a chic little suit. But Ellie had made sacrifices, and now her money had begun to mount up, especially since she'd let go the Kirribilli flat she'd shared with Mark, and moved further out of the city. Skipping lunch and forgoing drinks with friends after work had helped. She'd even given up the major vice that had driven Mark crazy of constantly buying new shoes with very high heels.

A quick costing from some infant catalogues had shown her just how expensive raising a child was likely to be, even without the childcare. Even if she was very frugal—and with Mark she'd learned to be *extremely* frugal—a safer car, as well as all the baby paraphernalia, would stretch her resources to the limit. The childcare would be the most difficult thing. It would all be much easier if she could bring the baby to work. Somehow, she would have to find a way to wangle that.

So, she reasoned, *plan*-wise, the advantages attached to becoming PA to Samos Stilakos far outweighed the risks.

She made practical preparations for the interview, determined to keep her reactions under control. If he gave her cool and impersonal, she'd give him super-efficient and remote. A man who couldn't remember her voice, or have any sense of her unique spiritual essence even after he'd slept with her, didn't deserve a drop of the Ellie O'Dea brand of personal warmth.

She rejected the idea of an expensive new suit, and chose a navy blue pinstripe her sister could no longer fit into. Tried and true, it looked dignified, even if the jacket was a little bulky on her and the skirt long. At least her last remaining pair of three-inch heels gave it some semblance of style. She rejected the sexy-camisole look for a crisp white shirt, loosely braided her hair into her nape, and was more than usually sparing with her perfume. If Samos Stilakos disliked secretaries who made their attraction to him obvious, she would give him nothing to complain of.

The interview got off to a disconcerting start. No other candidates waited with her in the outer office. After a lengthy wait, Caroline from HR—Caroline had waited too long and now had golden retrievers instead—emerged and gave her the nod.

With a pounding heart Ellie entered.

As tall, autocratic and darkly handsome as ever, Samos Stilakos was standing at his window, hands in his pockets, staring out. At the quiet sound of the door closing he turned, and her feet slowed to a halt. His dark eyes locked with hers across time and space, and she felt a dizzying whoosh, as though all the air were being sucked from the room.

The world held its breath, then Samos Stilakos moved, gesturing politely towards a chair with one lean, elegant hand, and she realised it was just that her lungs had forgotten to breathe.

The chair he'd indicated looked out on his Chief Executive

view of the harbour. He chose the chair opposite, so the light fell on her face, while his was in shadow. He murmured a few crisp words of greeting, then for a long, drawn-out minute scrutinised her, his dark eyes cool and impenetrable.

She waited, her nervous pulse ticking along until the sound of it swelled to fill the room.

After an eternity he said very softly, 'You have a piquant chin, Eleanor.'

The blood rushed to her cheeks. 'Really?' she said, struggling not to be thrown by a weird personal comment that had no place in a job interview. 'I hadn't noticed.'

What had he meant by it? Was it a criticism, or a compliment? Could a chin even *be* piquant?

He flicked her an enigmatic glance, then opened her CV and got down to the task of rigorously grilling her. She managed to answer his questions coolly and pleasantly, and hardly noticed his lean hands leafing through her personnel file.

Only once did she feel herself begin to slip into the mad craving she could have for him if she let herself go. It was during his line of questioning about her role on the Social Committee.

'I need my PA to be flexible, and not be afraid to show initiative,' he said in his deep, quiet voice. 'And you must realise, should you be successful in your application, that you won't have time to continue organising the staff parties.' He added drily, 'Of course, in the future there won't be so many to distract you.'

She gave a stiff nod. The stringent cuts to entertainment and the little luxuries of working life were sore points with the staff.

At that moment Samos Stilakos made a slight shift in position. She saw his trouser-leg ride up to expose a black sock. Beyond that black sock, her wanton imagination raced to envisage the hairy, muscular leg she knew resided inside the expensive fabric, and went on to roll out the whole, mouth-watering picture of bronzed, virile masculinity she remembered with such vivid power.

Without warning heat curled through her. Involuntarily her armpits and the palms of her hands moistened, and she felt her ears and other, more sensitive points grow hot.

'Are you finding it warm in here, Eleanor?' The deep polite voice cut through the steam of her flashback. 'Would you like some water?'

She met his cool enquiring glance and her flush deepened. 'No. No, thanks,' she said jerkily.

'Please,' he said, leaning forward, a dark gleam lighting his eyes, 'feel free to take off your jacket.'

She resisted that invitation, and somehow floundered the rest of the way through the interview, managing to keep all her clothes on, and to avoid any dangerous references to the masked ball.

She wasn't quite sure why, but a day later she had the job.

It was a tightrope, but not in the way Beth had predicted. Though Sam was always courteous and professional, a tension existed between them. When he was discussing projects with her, his deep, dark gaze intent on her face, sometimes she wondered if they were really talking about something else. Sometimes she felt his eyes dwelling on her face when he thought she wasn't aware.

At night she couldn't stop thinking about him, analysing everything that had happened between them during the day, even though she knew it was a dangerous weakness, and a path she mustn't travel.

And sometimes, right on the edge of sleep, at that moment when she had least control, she'd allow her mind to drift into wildly romantic fantasies, like the swooningly delicious one in which he'd acquired the bank solely because he'd fallen in love with her on the Night of Nights.

At work he smiled rarely, but when he did her insides were wrung. His deep, seductive voice swayed her concentration, and she had to fight to conceal her awareness of him behind a bland smile.

Though obviously she hadn't succeeded, she now realised

with a sinking heart. And he would be sure to have heard by now what Natalie had accused her of. Alice Springs beckoned, possibly even New Zealand.

She bent to search her bottom desk-drawer for the photo of Mark camping in the Pyrenees. Even after fourteen months she hadn't been ruthless enough to throw it away. At least he'd come in handy for something, even if it was only camouflage.

She sat it upright on her desk just as Sam's office door opened and his mother came out. She bid Ellie a friendly farewell, although Ellie thought she could read sympathy in the older woman's eyes.

The advice she always gave to juniors in trouble with their bosses was to never apologise, only explain. And to justify, justify, justify. But how would she ever explain this without giving everything away?

With a growing sense of dread, she made an attempt to get on with doing some strategic tweaking of Sam's latest presentation for the board. There was nothing wrong with his basic ideas, just that they were heavily weighted towards the bank's profits. Usually time just flew when she was editing one of her boss's projects. Now it was the longest ten minutes in history before the intercom buzzed.

'Come in, will you, Eleanor?' the deep, cool voice said.

With trembling hands Ellie whipped out her compact and made a quick inspection. Paler even than usual, and not at all mouse-like, but outwardly under control, apart from her hands and the slight dilation of her pupils. Her neck suddenly felt very sensitive, but if Anne Boleyn could face it, so could she.

A little unsteadily she rose, corrected the slight leftwards list of her Country Chic suit jacket—bought brand-new from a last season's seconds shop in Chinatown—and, head high, entered the office.

CHAPTER TWO

SAM at work was nothing like the Sam in a hotel bedroom.

Usually when Ellie came in he would be at his desk, writing, or frowning at spreadsheets. He would look up and watch her approach with that brooding, inscrutable gaze, then return to his work, silently motioning her to be seated.

This time she saw with foreboding that he was upright, his lean hips resting negligently against the massive rosewood desk, arms folded, waiting. He looked taller, his powerful shoulders wider. From across the room she saw his eyelids half lowered over watchful eyes as unreadable as the night.

She waded across the rich crimson carpet to him, conscious that his deep gaze was measuring every centimetre of her progress. She came to a halt a few metres short, her heart thumping against her ribs.

The silence thundered with her disgrace, though even in her suspense she couldn't help noticing the outline of his long powerful thighs, highlighted as his posture tugged on the fabric of his trousers.

'Ah, Eleanor,' he said with sinister, velvet charm. 'Please sit down.' He swept one bronzed, lean hand to indicate her usual chair.

'Thank you,' she said, shaky but resolute, 'but I'd prefer to stand.'

His black eyebrows twitched up. His eyes lit with a disquieting gleam. He shrugged. 'As you wish.' He straightened, strolled a few paces to the right, swung round to shoot a look at her, then strolled a few paces back.

Searching for the words, she supposed. He should have been good at it by now, with all his experience.

His foot crunched on something, and he kicked it aside and came to a halt. Ellie shifted nervously as his gaze seared down her vulnerable throat, to the fragment of lace revealed by her disobedient jacket, down to her brave but slightly tatty heels.

Sam felt an overwhelming desire to reach out and unbutton that jacket, but he repressed it. He wished he had X-ray vision to see the curves under the demure clothes, but at least the skin of her throat was the satin-white he remembered. He noted the small, betraying pulse there with a quick surge of satisfaction. It wasn't just him. Miss Ellie O'Dea wasn't quite as cucumber-cool as she pretended.

He lanced her with a glance that held just the right degree of professional sternness. 'I may have mentioned during your interview, Eleanor, the need in your job for absolute discretion.'

His deep voice sliced through the silence as easily as a sword through a tender neck.

Ellie's lashes fluttered down. This was it. The chop.

'Of course. You did mention it.' She braced herself, and plunged bravely in with, 'Is there something you want to say to me, Mr Stilakos? Because if there is something I need to explain, I'm sure I can satisfy you.'

He gazed meditatively at her for long seconds, his eyes narrowed, then said, 'I have no doubt of that, Eleanor. And, yes, there is something I want to say to you.' He strolled over to sit on the edge of his desk, and captured her eyes with his compelling glance. 'Until now things between us have been a little formal. I think you'll agree that the time has come for us to remove our masks.'

'Our—' The breath choked in Ellie's throat. 'What do you mean?'

The perceptive dark eyes scrutinising her face glinted. 'I

think you know exactly what I mean.' Her blood had just started a panicked rush to her head when he added in measured tones, 'A personal assistant has to be just that. *Personal.* If we're to work as a team our relationship needs to be closer. That means us getting to know each other. Being open with each other. I'm sure you have issues with me I know nothing about.'

Relief he was only using *masks* as a figure of speech made her so giddy she was seized with a rush of generosity. 'No, no, I don't. Well, not that many.' The attentive tilt of his dark head made her conscious of her soft words seeming to crash around the walls. 'I dare say everyone has his or her own management style.'

He grimaced. 'Good— I *think*. I hardly dare to ask, but are there some suggestions you'd like to offer? To help me improve my—performance?'

His eyebrows made an ironic twitch and the sternness of his beautiful, sexy mouth relaxed. Instantly her imagination flew her back to that lamp-lit bed where he reclined, bronzed, naked and wickedly intent on giving her the ultimate in pleasure, and a tidal surge of warmth swelled her breasts inside her cut-price bra.

'No, no,' she said, shaking her head to crush any suggestion of sexual innuendo. 'Of course not. I'm sure your performance—I mean your performance as a *boss*—is very good.'

He smiled. It was a rare event and she wished he hadn't. His eyes crinkled at the corners and seemed to lengthen charmingly. It made him devastatingly like the Sam of the hotel bedroom.

'Of course I knew you meant my performance as a boss,' he said softly. 'What else would I have thought you meant?' A shadow of the smile lingered as he contemplated her with a shimmering, intent gaze.

The suspicion crept into her head that he knew very well who she was and was toying with her. She twisted her boneless hands behind her back. Was he tempting her to flirt?

He began to pace again, only this time, to her intense confusion, *around* her. He circled, inspecting her as if she were a slave girl in some biblical market-place.

He prowled behind her and paused, and she stared straight ahead, embarrassment warring with her overwhelming physical awareness of him. What was he looking at? Suddenly she remembered a little fault she'd forgotten to fix in the pleat at the back of her skirt, and felt herself grow hot. She whipped around to face him, concealing her discomfiture with a touch of hauteur. 'Was there something else?'

'Tell me, Eleanor,' he said. 'Are you finding your salary adequate?'

'My salary?'

She nearly gasped. Her feminine pride was stung, though she knew there were those who would say she deserved to feel some shame. She was earning more than she'd even dreamed, and could easily have bought a new suit. Her bank balance had received such a boost that her savings fund was becoming quite healthy, but, she'd reasoned, in extreme circumstances a woman was forced to take extreme measures to protect herself.

'It's more than adequate, thanks,' she admitted. 'It's generous.'

He stood looking thoughtful for a second, then strode across to the desk and picked up the phone.

He dialled, unnerving her with a keen, meaningful glance. 'There is something of a deeply personal nature I need to discuss with you, but this isn't the place for it. I'm taking you to lunch. Payroll?' he said into the phone, then covered the mouthpiece with his hand and said, 'You'd better warn the restaurant upstairs we want a quiet table. And cancel our appointments for the afternoon.' With a brisk nod he turned back to his call. 'Jenkins? What do we pay Eleanor O'Dea?'

He waved her away, but as she headed for the door she had the sensation that his eyes were burning through the back of her suit.

'No,' she heard him tell Jenkins. 'Yes. No. No. Take it up. Make it twenty-five per cent. Better still, thirty.'

Outside the office door, Ellie stood for a moment, her mind in a whirl.

Something—*everything*—had changed. It appeared she wasn't getting the sack.

But what personal thing did he want to discuss? Surely not the night of the masked ball?

She dialled the penthouse restaurant, then stood rapidly reviewing their conversation. She still had her job, which suggested he hadn't remembered her. Though some of the things he'd said…

And there had been a definite buzz in the atmosphere. Whether he'd intended it or not his behaviour had been seductive. Charming, even. Although, if she was to be honest with herself, she always felt that zing in the air when she was near him. The question was whether it was all generated by her.

It was highly unlikely he'd flirt with her. Still, did a sophisticated man like Samos Stilakos use the word *relationship* accidentally? Somehow she doubted it.

Although…although…

This was the man who'd transferred four assistants for falling in lust with him, *and* sacked his Advertising Manager for conducting staff performance appraisals in the Honeymoon Suite at the Crown Regis, one of Sydney's most salubrious hotels. He'd never risk starting an affair with his PA after setting his workforce such an uncompromising example.

And what was this about her salary? Unless she'd misinterpreted that phone call, he intended giving her a raise. She thought back to that unsettling moment when he'd been prowling around her, and nearly groaned aloud. Beth had been right. She should have upgraded her wardrobe. What if the deeply personal thing he wanted to discuss with her was her suit?

Though anxiety gnawed at her vitals, she still made an effort to concentrate on the booklet she was preparing to support Sam's strategy for bringing the department heads around. Should she, or shouldn't she, include that fascinating research she'd uncovered about childcare in the workplace? Surely it was a prime opportunity to inform them of what they truly needed to know.

Sam's door opened and he strode out with his firm, energetic step. 'Ready?' His glance shifted past her and he halted. His eyes narrowed, and he strolled over to her desk and picked up Mark's photo. 'Who's this?' He turned a veiled glance on her face. 'Your boyfriend?'

'No, no. He's—a friend.' She supposed Mark could still be called a friend, even after fourteen months without a word. Certainly he hadn't wanted to be called a husband, or the father of her children.

Sam held up the photo to examine under the light, tilted it this way and that. 'There's something about him,' he commented, frowning. 'Reminds me of someone. Yes, I know. The woodsman in that story—what's it called?' He clicked his fingers. '*Hansel and Gretel*—that's the one. Does he always keep that beard?'

'He's a mountain climber. An—adventurer.'

He'd made Mark sound so ridiculous she couldn't help feeling a bit defensive. Although why should she? Mark had never been into haut couture. Her yearning for beautiful, elegant clothes had been one of the contentious issues between them, and she'd long since learned to suppress it. But there was nothing so ridiculous about a checked flannelette shirt, was there? Millions of men wore them.

'He likes—a challenge.' She'd been going to say *wide open spaces*, but the truth of that could still hit a nerve.

'Ah.' He shot her an inscrutable dark glance. 'Don't we all,' he said softly, and gave the photo a careful wipe with his immaculate Armani sleeve, before placing it on the desk directly in front of her chair. He flashed her a wicked smile. 'There. Now you can see him clearly. Ready now?'

He curved his arm around her back to escort her to the lift.

The revolving restaurant on the top floor was packed with the lunch-time crowd of executives and members of the public who wanted to enjoy spectacular views with their meals. She spotted several of Sirius's management staff, gossiping over their dry whites.

The news would be out in a flash, she thought, noting some curious heads turning their way as she made her entrance with Samos Stilakos. She could just hear them in the canteen—*Ellie is making it with the boss*. At least, though, with members of staff present he wasn't likely to spring any major surprises on her.

The *maître d'* swept all before him to lead them to a table in a discreet corner, magnificently set in white linen and crystal. 'Champagne, sir? Madam?' he said, after he'd seated them with a superb flourish of starched napery.

She was relieved when Sam said, his deep, quiet voice polite but commanding, 'Mineral water. This is a business meeting.'

Executives all over the restaurant hastened to conceal their wineglasses.

Sam gazed at her across the table, golden depths shimmering in his dark eyes, and her relief began to wane a little as her susceptible pulse picked up speed. 'Eleanor,' he said softly, ravishing her with a gleaming white smile. 'That's a Greek name. Did you know that?'

If only the smile didn't linger in his eyes like a caress. 'I thought it was French,' she answered, unable to prevent her own giddy smile from breaking out. 'You know, Eleanor of Aquitane and all that.'

'Eleanor of Aquitane was almost certainly of Greek descent,' he said. 'And I believe she also had strawberry hair.'

Strawberry. The word hit her like a thunderbolt and the smile was wiped from her face. If ever she'd needed proof of this man's pathetic memory here it was. Hadn't she provided him with a shining example of strawberry-blonde hair at the masked ball? On that occasion he'd displayed a passionate enthusiasm for plunging his hands into it, even burying his face in it. Having experienced it to the utmost, it was one colour he should have remembered.

It was glaringly apparent that to him all shades of red hair were the same. As no doubt all *women* looked the same.

'What is it?' His eyes lit with amusement and his thick black brows lifted. 'Have I said something?'

She concealed her chagrin behind the self-possessed demeanour she'd perfected for bosses over the years. 'I believe Eleanor of Aquitane was one-hundred-per-cent French,' she replied coolly. 'And my hair colour is usually described as Titian.'

His lean, handsome face betrayed no expression. 'Oh, is it? Titian. I must remember that.' He looked so solemn she had the strongest suspicion that for some reason he was pleased with himself, and trying not to show it. He motioned to her to open her menu, and perused his while she made a pretence of reading.

Food words danced meaninglessly in front of her eyes. Why were they discussing her personal attributes? Next he'd be bringing up her piquant chin. If she didn't know better, at any minute now she'd be expecting a sexy little après-lunch invitation down to the Crown Regis.

A nasty suspicion occurred to her. Perhaps he always seduced his PAs over lunch. Maybe that was why he then had to banish them to the ends of the earth.

She hated to believe it, but it fitted. Why hadn't she realised? For months the staff had speculated about those transfers. No one had had any doubt that the women had earned them with their unprofessional behaviour. But what if *he* had been the seducer? When he turned on his devilish charm he was impossible to resist, as she could testify only too well.

With growing disappointment she surveyed the handsome, inscrutable face absorbed in reading the menu. A serial sacker was one thing, but a serial womaniser quite another. For some reason she'd needed to believe in his integrity. What did it say about her, that she'd spent the night with someone like him?

'A lovely name,' he murmured. 'And yet—' He looked up to capture her gaze. 'You invite people to call you Ellie.'

She looked enquiringly at him over the top of her menu.

'Your friends.'

'Yes?'

'But not your boss.'

She was momentarily flustered. A smile warmed his dark

eyes, crept into her veins and stole down her arteries like old cognac. She forced herself to keep on breathing as if it were an everyday experience for her to be teased by tall, dark, dangerous Greeks with beautiful, sexy mouths that curled up at the corners.

'I'd prefer it if you would drop the *Mr Stilakos* routine, and just call me Sam,' he added gently.

There was a pregnant silence while he waited for her to reply in kind. It was fortunate that just then a waiter materialised beside their table. She wasn't hungry, but she welcomed the lad as if he were her saviour, bathing him in her warmest smile. 'I'll have the salad, thanks,' she told him.

She was conscious of Sam leaning back in his chair, his long limbs idly disposed, his gaze flickering over her as he listened to the small exchange. When it was his turn he ordered the fish, and in a few brief words gave detailed instructions in exactly how it was to be prepared. After the waiter left, he moved his chair a little closer and said quietly, 'I'm wondering, Eleanor, if your friend will be able to spare you for a weekend, just over a month from now.'

A million unlikely scenarios raised their heads. 'Beth?' she said, taken off guard.

'Your friend. The *adventurer*.' Somehow he managed to invest the word with a subtle mockery.

'Oh, Mark?' She gave a small self-conscious laugh and mumbled, 'No, no. Well, he's not— He's not actually—' She folded her napkin carefully, folded it into smaller and smaller rectangles. She'd never intended to lie about Mark's presence in her life, only to divert suspicion. What if she had to produce him at some time? It would be so humiliating to be caught in a lie. Quickly she backed away from it. 'Why? What's happening?'

She felt his perceptive eyes home in on her nervous fingers, and forced them to stay still.

'So you'll be free?' There was a gleam in his eyes that suggested he hadn't been fooled by her little strategy.

Her heart lurched. Was he about to suggest a weekend rendezvous? For a wavering instant she allowed a shining mirage to float in her imagination—the two of them, making love in some decadent, luxurious hotel.

Despicable. Fatal. But such sweet poison. If the others hadn't resisted, how would she?

Breathlessly she replied, 'It depends what for.'

He hesitated. 'You met my mother this morning…'

She nodded, hypnotised by his mesmeric gaze.

'My mother has to go to a family wedding. Her heart isn't very strong and she finds she's nervous about having to go on her own. I wondered if I could impose on your good nature to ask if you would consider going with her?'

His *mother*! She nearly fell off the chair. This was nothing like she'd expected. Inviting her to a social function with his mother, his family—!

Her suspicions all fell in a heap. How could she have been so cynical? And foolish, suspecting him of seducing his PAs, even worrying about what he thought of her clothes when he'd probably never even noticed them. As for her fanciful dream of an afternoon of wild sex down at the Regis… She should have blushed with shame.

'Of course, I'll make sure you're handsomely reimbursed for your time and trouble.'

She pulled herself together. 'Why me?' she said. 'Why not you, or another family member, or a friend?'

He sat back. His lean, strong face hardened to become expressionless. 'It's a family affair. I don't know if you know anything about the Stilakos family—'

Only what everyone knew, that they owned a bank, half the media outlets in the country, and controlling interests in several trans-global corporations besides Sirius. She wasn't about to acknowledge what she knew of the personal stuff shooting along the office airways, and shook her head.

'It's my ex-wife, Natalie, who's getting married. You'll have met her this morning. She's marrying—another family member.'

There'd been a hesitation, so slight as to be barely perceptible, but his dark eyes hardened to obsidian. 'On my mother's side.'

Ellie had a vague recollection of some scandal about Natalie a few years ago. While the star had been well known because of her television fame and wild-child reputation, at that time her husband's name had meant nothing to Ellie.

'As you might imagine, everyone in the family, all the *friends* of the family, are in some way involved with the bride and groom. You probably noticed this morning, Natalie can be temperamental…'

She gave a noncommittal shrug.

He laughed. 'Always the diplomat, Eleanor.'

A pleasant, unexpected glow irradiated her insides. Perhaps she should forgive him for forgetting her. After all, a man like him had serious things on his mind.

'Natalie can be—just a little volatile. Weddings are emotional affairs, and my mother is nervous of the possibilities. If she had some calm, sensible person with her, some neutral person, I think she might feel more confident.'

'You—haven't been invited ?' she hazarded.

His eyes darkened, and became so impenetrable she had the heart-gripping sensation she'd tripped a detonator wire set to blow her sky-high. For goodness' sake, why had she asked? Of course people didn't go to their ex's weddings.

'It's probably better you don't go,' she hastened to say. 'It would be sure to arouse painful memories.' His face remained tense, and she strove to lighten the tone with humour. 'I imagine the last thing anyone would want on their wedding day would be their ex turning up at the church. All their friends sitting on the edges of their pews… Everyone waiting for hell to break loose. I can see it all now—' she raised a solemn hand and intoned in a priestly voice '"—if any man here knows of any reason why this man should avoid marrying this woman…"'

To her relief his taut face relaxed and he broke into a laugh. 'It may surprise you to know I have been invited. My ex-wife has infinite faith in my ability to keep my mouth shut. She begs me to come.' He added drily, 'That's what you were hearing this morning. Natalie persuading me.'

He smiled, but Ellie felt a little chill thrill down her spine. There were jagged depths beneath that brooding calm. She would hate to be the one who disturbed them.

'What do you think?' He scanned her face for a moment, then lowered his black lashes and said, 'This doesn't mean your job is on the line if you refuse, Eleanor. This is apart from your work. It's personal, and I'll understand and accept it immediately if you choose not to be involved.'

She'd been wrong. Absolutely wrong on all counts. The man wasn't a scoundrel in any way. He was a concerned, affectionate son willing to go out on a limb for his mother, even if it meant exposing his personal skeletons to a stranger. A mere employee!

The waiter arrived with the meals, and she took advantage of the distraction to think.

How she'd misjudged him. It was sobering to see how close she'd come to turning into a cynic in her old age. She looked up to meet his dark, velvet gaze and her heart warmed. What a relief to be able to think well of him. 'All right,' she said, smiling. 'I'll do it. If you're sure your mother will be comfortable with me.'

His eyes lit with satisfaction. 'Good.' He took up his knife and fork and added, 'I've phoned her and she thinks she will be. Now, eat up your salad. We'll need to see her and do some shopping. And we'll need to discuss the travel arrangements.'

Ellie raised her brows.

'Didn't I mention it? Natalie's parents live on the Gold Coast. The wedding's at the Palazzo Versace. You'll be staying there.'

Ellie was dazzled. The Palazzo Versace was supposedly one of the glitziest resorts in the country. She tried to remember what she'd heard of it. Television ads she'd seen had left her with vague impressions of a glittering palace floating on a moonlit lagoon; beautiful languid people, lounging on luxurious chaises longues, sipping piña coladas. She could easily imagine Natalie there, but could Ellie O'Dea be one of those people?

'Great,' she said doubtfully.

'You might need to take your swimsuit,' he said, considering her over the rim of his glass. 'Just because it's a wedding doesn't mean you have to suffer the whole time. There're bound to be things you can do to pass the time while my mother catches up with her family—beaches, sailing, wind-surfing—you know the sort of thing…' He made a careless gesture with one lean, bronzed hand, then paused, contemplating her with an intent shimmering gaze.

'I'm not much of a one for beaches,' she confessed. 'I have to avoid too much sun.'

His eyes flickered to her throat. 'Ah, yes. I can see that. You are very fair, aren't you? So you never go to the beach?'

Ellie felt herself grow warm. This was too reminiscent of a conversation she'd had with him before in quite a different setting. Was it a coincidence that so many of the things he'd said to her since ten o'clock that morning in some way recalled the Night of Nights?

She gazed searchingly at him. 'Early mornings, or—or late afternoons are fine. I do like to swim. Sometimes I—' she waved her hand in a stiff gesture '—use the pool at the gym.'

'As I recall, there is quite a lovely pool at that resort. A spa, no less.'

'I'm not sure I can imagine myself at that sort of place.' She gave a small laugh.

'*I* can imagine it,' he said softly. A gleam lit his dark eyes. 'I can imagine it very well.' He looked silently at her for a long minute that grew longer and more deafening by the second as questions danced again in Ellie's brain. 'And there is always the night,' he murmured, still gazing at her.

She stared back at him in amazement. 'The night?' Her voice

came out deeper than she expected; it sounded almost croaky. 'I don't think I'd feel safe on the beach at night.'

His eyebrows went up, then he laughed, a low, sexy laugh. 'Wouldn't you? But what if you were with someone?'

Her heart skipped a major beat while her lashes fluttered in shock. 'Who? You mean…someone I met at the wedding?'

His eyes chilled and his fork arrested in mid-air. 'I certainly didn't mean that.' He pinned her with a severe gaze. 'Try to remember this, Eleanor. You'll be there to keep my mother company, not for the sake of a hot weekend.' He must have seen her dismay because he added, his deep, smooth voice rich with charm, 'Though, of course, I know you aren't the type of person to ditch your responsibilities for a fling with some stranger.' He smiled at her, and turned his attention back to his meal while her head buzzed with indignant thoughts. *He* wasn't above a fling with a stranger. So why even mention it? Why, unless he was giving her some sort of signal?

She stared at her barely touched salad. All at once the uncertainty became too much. What sort of a pathetic coward was she to allow this cat-and-mouse game to continue?

If he sacked her, he sacked her.

'Look, Sam…' She took a deep breath and on a rush of bravado leaned forward and murmured in a voice just above a whisper, 'Are you—are you by any chance referring to the night of the masked ball?'

As soon as the words were out a blush the size of a tsunami swamped her. She clenched her entire body and held her breath.

Across the table Sam's bronzed hands stilled. She lifted her gaze and met his brilliant dark eyes. They were gleaming with a deeply unsettling intensity.

He spoke so quietly she had to strain to hear him above her madly thundering heartbeat. 'I'm not referring to it,' he said. 'I'm very carefully not. If you want me to discuss it, you'll have to release me from my promise, won't you, Eleanor?'

Relief washed through her. Impossibly, she felt the colour

deepen in her cheeks. 'Oh. Well, of course, of course. I *do*…
There's no point… I'm certainly not trying to…'

'Good. I'd hate to think we'd come this far for nothing.'

Her nerves jumped in shock. *We'd come this far…?*
Towards…what?

Sam Stilakos laid down his knife and fork. When her glance
fell on his hands she noticed that they weren't quite steady.

The waiter came with fresh water, creating such a welcome
diversion she and Sam both hastened to chat warmly with him.
After the boy had gone, Sam lounged back in his chair and said
idly, 'So who is this boyfriend? What's-his-name—Tim?'

'Oh. You must be meaning—Mark.'

His thick black lashes screened his gaze while she gathered
herself to reply. She drained her glass and took her time refill-
ing it from the carafe, then said with a careful lack of expression, 'Mark went to Antarctica.'

His brows lifted and he scanned her face. 'Antarctica! For a
holiday—or…?'

She rearranged her salad. 'An expedition.'

His brows went up again. 'Ah. And do you—*when* do you—
expect him back?'

She shrugged. 'Oh, some time,' with an airy wave of her
hand. She didn't want to let on how long he'd been gone. And
that he'd since been seen in Melbourne with a blonde whose
idea of couture was to wear army boots with a denim skirt.

Samos Stilakos continued to study her face with a veiled
gaze. After a long moment he remarked in a low, musing voice,
'Antarctica. That's a long way from here.'

CHAPTER THREE

'I THINK you've been in this car, Eleanor, haven't you?'

The lazy enquiry rocked Ellie on her heels just as she was about to get into Sam's Porsche. Of course she'd been in it. He'd driven her in it to Circular Quay, and kissed her long and lingeringly as the first rays of dawn had ignited Sydney Harbour in a sunburst of molten ecstasy. It had been the highlight of her life to date.

'Remind me again,' he said, flashing her a glance through his black lashes, 'which do you prefer? Roof open, or closed?'

Smiling, she indicated her hair. 'What do you think?'

He strode around to the driver's side and lowered his long frame into the seat next to hers. His hand moved to the gear stick, and she instinctively shifted her knees, although of course she knew he wouldn't have touched them. Not this time.

But it was far too reminiscent of the last time, when he'd driven her to the ferry terminal in the sweet haze of afterglow. Then, the city streets, the very air she'd breathed, had seemed intoxicating. It was intoxicating *now*, sitting beside him as he threaded a path through the traffic with breathtaking efficiency, his beautiful hands relaxed on the wheel.

No wonder Schanelle and the others had ogled him.

Scorchingly conscious of him in the confined space, she tried to restrain herself, but somehow her eyes were drawn to drink in his sexy mouth, so grave in repose. A suggestion of shadow on his firm, lean jaw evoked a stirring memory of his early-morning face, nuzzling a bristly imprint on her tender skin.

'Something wrong?' he said, turning his head suddenly and catching her.

'No, no,' she said, flushing a little. 'I was just—er—thinking about Schanelle.'

'Ah. Now there's a coincidence.'

Her heart plunged to the floor. Could she be going insane? Whatever had possessed her to remind him of poor Schanelle? But he made a sudden swift lane-change, executed a heart-stopping but brilliantly adroit U-turn in the face of oncoming traffic, and drew the car to a smooth standstill at the kerb.

She stared confusedly out, and saw they were parked in front of a boutique with elegant lettering across its large, black-framed windows. 'Oh, the *shop*.'

He cast her an amused glance. 'You know this shop, of course.'

'From the outside,' she admitted with a grin, surmising they were here so he could choose a wedding present for his ex-wife. 'I'll wait in the car.'

'No, you will not,' he asserted. He sprang out and strode around to open her door, forcing her out with a firm, expectant gaze.

She stood uncertainly on the pavement in front of the entrance. How did he think she would be able to help? PAs with savings targets didn't shop in places like this.

'Come on.' He took her arm and manoeuvred her inside.

A severely smart shop assistant, with sleek blonde hair and emphatic eye-liner, registered his approach with an open mouth. Ellie wished a fly would buzz in, until she remembered her own first sighting and forgave her.

'We need things for a weekend wedding,' Sam told the woman, seemingly not put off by prolonged eye contact. 'Dresses, suits, shoes. Swimsuits. Size…' He turned a suave glance on Ellie. 'I'm guessing ten. Would that be right, Eleanor?'

Ellie dragged her eyes away from a shelf of fabulously high shoes with jewelled heels. 'What? *I* don't need anything.'

'Yes, you do,' he said. 'I can't plunge you into this without providing you with the necessary equipment. I've been through this kind of thing and I've learned the hard way about what's expected of women. You'll need dresses, shoes, handbags...' He began ticking a list off on his fingers. 'An outfit to be seen arriving in, casual things to lounge around in, things for daytime, evening, the church, and we mustn't forget the swimming.'

Ellie nearly tottered on her heels. She stared at him, then around at all the lovely creations poking from their racks. This attitude was absolutely the opposite of Mark's, who believed elegant clothes to be the trappings of empty vanity. It was religion with Mark that money should only be spent on functional items, like hiking boots and thermal underwear.

This was generosity on a scale she'd never encountered, but deep down she knew she couldn't accept it. She was a free and independent woman, and, whatever else Sam was, he was her boss.

She angled herself away from the interested stare of the saleswoman and mumbled, 'I have things I can wear.'

She felt the assistant's experienced eye assess her clumsy jacket and skirt, and tried to look cool and unconcerned, though she could feel her face turning pink.

'I know you do,' Sam said soothingly, 'but for this you'll need new things. Show us everything you've got,' he instructed the woman over Ellie's head.

Dollar signs danced in front of Ellie's eyes while the woman jumped to obey the command in his voice. Ellie watched helplessly as she reefed through the racks and pulled out hanger after hanger of gorgeous, to-die-for outfits, any of which would leave a massive hole in her savings.

'This is not the sort of thing I wear,' Ellie protested, waving away a purple suit with a short slim skirt. For the price on its label she could probably furnish a nursery and pay for five years of violin lessons.

Sam looked surprised. 'Isn't it? I think it'd look good on you. Try it on.'

She shook her head, 'This is very kind of you, but I don't *need* you to buy me anything, thanks.' She met his gaze steadily. 'I really can't accept this.'

Disconcerted, Sam stared at her, wondering if he was losing his grip. A delicate flush washed her flawless cheeks and disappeared into her hairline. There was a smile on her soft mouth, but her blue eyes were resolute. He felt a curious jolt, and was reminded of another time he'd come up against a brick wall with Ellie O'Dea. But surely none of the women he'd ever known would have refused clothes from this establishment.

He gestured to the saleswoman to turn her attention to other customers, and ushered Ellie to a quiet corner. It took him a moment to find the words. 'Let me explain, Eleanor.'

That deep, persuasive tone could melt steel, and Ellie braced herself for a major charm offensive, but the dark velvet eyes scanning hers were sincere.

'I don't wish to insult you,' he said carefully, 'but you don't know Natalie and her friends. You'll be competing in the most cutthroat market in the country. You'll need to wear something swish, or risk feeling uncomfortable. I can't just drop you in it. My mother would kill me.' He smiled and wrapped a reassuring arm around her, and every cell in her body surged. 'It isn't a big deal. Relax. I have to do this, believe it.'

The dark seductive resonance of his voice went straight to her head. Through the fabric of his suit she felt the heat of his large, lean body, and her blood went zinging on a dizzy dangerous course to her breasts and points south.

'You're—you're really very kind.' She quickly disengaged herself. Her ears felt as if they'd caught fire. She met the sensual awareness vibrant in his dark gaze, and knew he'd noticed her quick pull away, and understood the reason.

'Honestly, Sam,' she rushed to fill the awkward moment, 'this is too generous of you.' Her heart was racing, but she forced herself to keep her head. He was so persuasive. Beautiful things called to her from every direction, but to allow him to buy even one dress for her would be shameful, when she could very well buy something for herself. 'I don't need a whole new wardrobe just for one weekend. If I need a dress, I can buy it myself.' She made a small dismissive wave towards a shelf where shoes kept flashing in the corner of her eye like hot magnets. 'Or—or shoes, or whatever.'

His black brows knitted, and she could tell by the calculation in his gaze that he wasn't about to give in. 'Er…' He turned to glance around the shop in search of inspiration.

Suddenly he turned back to her, a gleam in his eyes. 'All right. Let's compromise. We don't want to offend these people, now, do we? You can't leave without at least trying something on. How about some of those shoes?'

Who was he, the devil? She glanced at them once, then averted her eyes. Somehow he'd homed straight in on her Achilles heel.

She shook her head and gave a small, reluctant laugh. 'You're very cunning.'

His eyes glinted. 'I *am* very cunning, and you'd do well to remember that, Eleanor. Go on. Try some.'

She looked over at the shoes. She could resist chocolate if she absolutely had to, for life-preserving reasons, but this was too much. She wasn't sure how it was a compromise, but with her blood churning like an excitable sea, she started with the shoes, and it wasn't long before two sales assistants were plying her with the clothes.

Obviously experienced with the ways of women in dress shops, Sam found an alcove with a pile of newspapers and dropped into a chair.

Ellie tried on the purple suit, and saw it accentuate her curves and turn her eyes to violet. The saleswoman brought her more suits, frothy skirts and evening dresses in rich colours with beads and sequins—jeans, swimsuits, even bikinis. Despite her initial reluctance, the fever for lovely things gripped her. There was a time for being frugal, she acknowledged to herself, and

a high society wedding wasn't one of them. She had to accept
that he knew what he was talking about. She did need at least
one good dress. She would just have to make an adjustment to
her IVF timeline.

Several times the woman dragged her to a large mirror outside
the cubicle. Sam lounged across the room, buried in his newspa-
per, though once Ellie glanced towards him in the mirror and felt
a small shock as she met his intent gaze.

'If madam would try these,' the saleswoman suggested,
handing Ellie some extremely frivolous shoes with four-inch
heels. She'd just finished zipping a short-sleeved dress, in a
shade of pink so delicate it was nearly white. Cut to classiç per-
fection, it moulded slinkily to her curves, emphasising the
perky up-tilt of her breasts. The shade lent her pale skin a
pearly glow, and her blue eyes sparkled like sea water. She
examined herself in it with delight, feeling as if she could
slither like a snake. She slid into the shoes, and her legs length-
ened with the old fabulous miracle.

'I *love* this,' she admitted, twisting in the small cubicle to
examine her derrière. 'It isn't too tight, is it?'

'No, no!' the woman cooed. 'It's made for you. Come
outside and see.'

The saleswomen whisked her out to the big mirror and fluttered around her. One stood on tiptoes and tried to rearrange
her hair. 'How does it look out?'

She tried to explain that if it wasn't severely bound up it just
fell straight, like a heavy curtain. She put her hands up to loosen
it, knowing she was surrendering to more than letting her hair
fall. For once she'd be breaking the embargo on her savings.
But hadn't she been given a pay rise by the most generous boss
a woman could ever…?

Her eyes slewed towards him in the mirror, and did a
double take.

Far from being sprawled in his chair, he was sitting bolt
upright, his big frame taut, his burning gaze riveted on her, as if

on some vision. A thrill shocked through her at the concentrated wolfish expression of his lean, strong face. She felt his eyes sear her from head to toe, their electric message unmistakable.

Her mouth dried. Transfixed, she watched him drop the paper and rise to his feet.

'We'll take it,' he growled, striding purposefully across to her without shifting his gaze. 'And the shoes. Let me help you with that, Eleanor.'

The assistants fell back to give him space. He raised his hands to her hair, and she felt the sensual charge in his smooth fingers frisson in her skin as they coupled with hers to release the pins. Her nape, her scalp, the length of her spine tingled as his strong, lean fingers plunged into her hair. After a wild few moments in which her pulse roared through her veins like whitewater rapids, he stood back to let the red silken mass fall free.

His hands gripped her shoulders and he held her to her reflection, a flame in his eyes. 'Look at you,' he said, gravel in his deep voice. 'You look perfect. Absolutely perfect.'

Her eyes glittered back at her from the mirror with a bluer intensity. His searing gaze locked with hers, their desire as seductive and compelling as it had been in that hotel room, and her breasts surged in a deep, responsive excitement. She felt a dizzy tide of unreality, as if she weren't in a shop with her boss, but with her lover in some private moment, on the verge of an explosive flare-up of passion.

But…he wasn't her lover. Not now and never again. Whatever images glowed in their memories were just that. Memories.

Restraining what felt like a natural compulsion to turn and embrace him, she lowered her lashes. 'I—I'd better take it off.' She made a move towards the fitting room.

'No,' he breathed. 'Leave it on.' His grip tightened for an instant before he released her. 'It's—ideal for where we're going next,' he said gruffly. A faint tinge of colour darkened his olive tan.

He swung abruptly away from her. She slipped back into the fitting room and took some deep, trembling breaths in an attempt to compose herself. One of the saleswomen came in to remove the labels from her dress, and took away the items she'd put on the possibles pile.

Ellie plunged into her bag for her hairbrush and did a quick tidy-up, her rapid heart thudding. She wasn't sure how she was going to face him when she came out. Something had happened between them, something irrevocable. Could they just pretend it hadn't?

She could hear the murmur of his deep voice in conversation with the saleswoman. 'We'll take them all,' she heard him say. 'And throw in all the matching shoes, et cetera.'

Though her poise was barely recovered, nonetheless her pride came roaring back.

'No! Wait.'

She burst from the fitting room, and hurried over to insert herself between Sam and the startled assistant. 'I'll take this dress and these shoes I'm wearing now,' she told the woman. She whipped her credit card from her purse, and pushed Sam's aside to lay hers on the counter. 'These are all I need,' she said with a firm glance at him, 'and *I* want to buy them. But thanks, anyway, for your most generous offer.' She smiled and added softly, 'I really do appreciate it.'

Something flickered in his intent dark gaze, and his brows knitted, but he must have seen the resolution in her face, because he stood back and allowed her to complete the transaction without argument. The assistant wrapped her work clothes and old shoes in tissue, and slipped them into stylish carrier bags.

She floated hazily beside him to the car in her chic little sexy dress and shoes, still in something of a turmoil. She'd expected a bigger fight over the matter of payment. Nonetheless, though she was still reeling at the price, it was a victory to have out-argued an autocrat who had an entire workforce quaking in its boots.

But there was the other thing. That moment in the shop.

He'd hardly spoken a word since, and, though he seemed as

assured as ever, she had the feeling he was as burningly conscious of it as she was herself. It was hard to meet his eyes, but when she did they brimmed with satisfaction, and something more. Something very akin to the desire she'd seen in that mirror.

The trip in the car was surprisingly brief. She'd thought they were heading for the bridge, when, against all her expectations, he swung the Porsche into the driveway of a grand hotel. She craned her neck, trying to read the inscription over the portico. Wasn't this the—?

The doors were opened by uniformed valets. 'Welcome to the Crown Regis, Mr Stilakos.' And with a deep bow. 'Madam.'

CHAPTER FOUR

SAM ushered her into the marble lobby. The concierge, the porters—everyone greeted him by name.

'Wait here a moment,' he said, steering her towards a plush velvet sofa.

Ellie stood still, besieged by doubts. Hadn't he said he would take her to visit his mother? She watched him stride across to Reception, and lean over to murmur something to the receptionist, who picked up the phone, spoke briefly, then handed him something.

Ellie's pulse quickened. She thought she could guess what it was.

In a second he was back, his eyes glinting when they lighted on her like a wolf with his prey in sight. With a light touch on her arm he guided her to the lifts. This was the time to call a halt. But what mature, twenty-nine year old woman would refuse to allow the most thrilling lover she'd ever known to escort her to the Honeymoon Suite of Sydney's most salubrious hotel?

In the lift they stood slightly apart, watching the floor count on the display panel, Ellie's heart in a dilemma, rapids churning in her veins. What was she doing?

'She's expecting us,' he said as the floor count reached thirty-five.

'Who? Oh. Do you mean then—? Your mother is staying *here*?'

He glanced down at her, his devilish brows raised. 'Of

course. Didn't I say? She always stays here when she comes up to town. Why else would we be here, Eleanor?'

The doors opened then, sparing her the impossibility of replying. Either she was a horribly confused woman, or her imagination had just taken her overboard. Or—Samos Stilakos was playing a game with her. A flirty, tantalising and very sexy game!

His mother opened her door to them and greeted them both warmly, although she regarded Ellie with faint surprise in her eyes.

'You've met Eleanor, Mother,' Sam said, with a glance at Ellie. 'I think she might be the person you're looking for.'

Ellie held out her hand. 'Hello, Mrs Stilakos.'

'Call me Irene,' the older woman said, taking her hand and looking her over with admiration. 'You look so nice. Is that how you were wearing your hair this morning?'

Ellie shook her head, conscious of Sam's eyes on her.

'Eleanor's hair was meant to flow free,' he stated.

She nearly gasped, wondering what Irene made of this, but the older woman merely beamed. 'And it does suit you. Come through, Eleanor.'

'*Ellie*, please.'

Sam's eyebrows twitched ironically at that, but he was silent as they followed his mother through to the suite's elegant sitting room. Irene showed them to winged chairs beside a large window, which overlooked the harbour and the Opera House. Other windows revealed different aspects of the city, sparkling in the afternoon haze. It might not have been the Honeymoon Suite, but it was certainly appealing.

Irene sat facing them on a crimson sofa. She'd changed from her chic morning suit to casual trousers and a dusty-pink top, and her hair was slightly flattened on one side, as if she'd recently woken from a midday snooze. With the light from the window on her face, Ellie could see lines of tiredness around her eyes and mouth.

'I'm so glad Sam had the brilliant idea of asking you, Ellie. Eleanor…' She tilted her head to one side. 'Is that a family name?'

Ellie could feel Sam's interested gaze on her face as she responded to Irene. 'My parents named us all after queens. One of my sisters is Cleopatra. There's an Isabella, and a Liz, of course, and I was called after Eleanor of Aquitane.'

'All very powerful women,' Irene nodded approvingly. 'Are your sisters married?'

Ellie found herself describing her family, including her father's work in the music department at Newcastle University, and her parents' rambling home on Lake Macquarie.

'Do all your sisters have children?'

Ellie nodded. 'Nearly all.'

'I bet you make a lovely auntie, Ellie.'

Ellie smiled. 'I do my best,' she admitted, although she didn't acknowledge her understanding of what this little fishing expedition was all about. Not with its unwary subject sitting right there in all his lazy drop-dead gorgeousness. She wondered if she would be like this with *her* sons? Always on the lookout for an eligible wife and mother for the grandchildren?

If she had sons, she thought with a small anxious pang. If there was an egg left by the time she could afford it!

Still, Irene's skills in helping her to relax, while extracting information from her about her family in the gentlest, least offensive way imaginable, were impressive.

There was so much one could learn from an older woman, she mused. Unless the older woman's son was sitting across from her, dripping with sexual charisma and soaking up every word.

'Mum! For God's sake,' he growled when Irene's curiosity threatened to go too far, and occasionally he rolled his eyes or exchanged an amused glance with Ellie, but she could feel his sharp intelligence weighing everything she said.

She had a slight respite when a knock came at the door, and Sam got up. A waiter wheeled in a table swathed in white linen, and set with Wedgwood china. Clever little warming drawers inserted underneath held a feast of toasted sandwiches, scones and a fluffy passionfruit sponge.

At Sam's insistence, Ellie accepted a toasted sandwich of baked ham and avocado. 'You don't know how long it will be before you get your dinner tonight, Eleanor,' he said. 'You'll need to keep your strength up.'

Tonight. She looked quickly at him. The dark eyes dwelling on her face were veiled, his sculpted mouth grave. She felt the heat rise in her cheeks. She took a small bite, but, delicious though it was, her appetite seemed to have deserted her.

Irene's bright gaze swung from one to the other of them, then she busied herself in pouring the tea. Ellie wondered how attuned the older woman was to picking up vibrations.

'I don't know how much Sam has told you about the wedding, Ellie,' she said. She inclined towards Ellie and confided, 'I'm afraid it might turn out to be quite dramatic.'

Sam's mouth curled wryly. 'Eleanor *has* met Natalie, Mum.'

'Well, I hope Ellie doesn't think I'm a coward.' Irene smiled at her. 'Milk?' She handed her a cup and saucer. 'Tea, Sam?' He waved a refusal, and she continued, 'I'm not really nervous. I love weddings, and I'm so looking forward to seeing my brother and his wife—the whole family! It's just that I like to have someone to talk to when I'm travelling.'

'Of course,' Ellie responded warmly. 'I understand exactly. No one likes travelling alone. Especially to weddings, where everything is about couples.'

Sam lounged back in his chair, his smooth, lean hands idle. Ellie could feel his dark gaze from beneath his sleepily lowered lashes scorching a pathway of sensual masculine interest from her Titian hair all the way down to her ankles.

Irene continued to give an excellent impersonation of a woman with energy to spare. 'That's true,' she agreed, her grey eyes sparkling behind her specs. 'And that's how you feel, don't you, dear?' she said earnestly to Sam, whose slumbrous gaze snapped into startled focus. 'A man without a woman is always twice as suspect at a wedding.'

Sam looked thunderstruck, but his mother ignored it, turning animatedly to Ellie. 'I knew you'd understand, Ellie. You and I'll get along perfectly.' She loaded a scone with cream. 'I'll let my brother know you're coming. And I'm sure you won't have any trouble with Natalie. She'll have so much on her mind she won't even notice you're there.'

'What?' Sam demanded, recovering. 'Why should Ellie—*Eleanor*—have trouble?'

Ellie's heart skipped an anxious beat for fear of what Irène might say, but she merely leaned over and patted her son's knee. 'No need to be alarmed, Sam. Ellie will be quite safe.' She gave Ellie a conspiratorial glance and said with a small, nervous laugh, 'If it comes to a showdown, Ellie and I can defend ourselves. We aren't scared, are we?'

'A showdown?' Sam's eyebrows shot up and he turned a sharp gaze from his mother to Ellie. 'What sort of a showdown? Why should anyone be scared?'

'Don't you worry at all, dear,' Irene said, her voice quavering a little. 'This is secret women's business. We don't need any men to protect us, do we, Ellie?'

Sam scoured their faces in such bemusement Ellie found it hard not to laugh.

As if in total innocence of the effect she was having on her son's peace of mind, Irene continued, 'Now, Ellie, you won't have to be stuck with me the whole time. I'll probably be gallivanting about with my relations for quite a lot of it.'

Sam shot his mother a quick frowning glance, but Irene went on, 'You're bound to meet up with someone your own age you can have fun with, isn't she, Sam? There's so much to do on the Coast.'

Ellie gave a noncommittal laugh. 'Either way is fine with me. I'm sure I'll find something to do if you're not around.'

She felt Sam's dark gaze searing a hole through her skull.

His eyes were narrowed, and there was a sardonic little curve to his lips. 'What might you do, Eleanor? Planning on taking a good book?'

'Perhaps.' She gazed coolly back at him, refusing to let him mock her in front of his mother. 'Perhaps not.'

Irene glanced at each of them, and said brightly, 'Well, it won't worry you whatever Ellie does, will it, dear, because you won't be there.' She beamed at him and turned to Ellie. 'Michael—he's the groom—is a keen yachtsman, like Sam, and I believe some of his young friends from the yacht club are sailing up there in advance of the wedding. The Palazzo Versace has a marina, so you might have an opportunity to do some sailing.'

Sam frowned. 'Sailing would be a mistake for Eleanor,' he said, in cool, clipped tones, his gaze on Ellie's face. 'She can't afford to get sunburnt.'

'Nonsense, Sam,' Irene exclaimed. 'She doesn't have to be wearing a tiny little bikini like some of them do, but if she does want to there's always sunscreen. And I'm sure you'd look lovely in it,' she added with a warm glance at Ellie.

Ellie felt the blood rise in her cheeks as the vision of her bikini-clad self dangled in the air.

'The jury's still out on the efficacy of sunscreen,' Sam said, holding her pink face under the spotlight of his sensual dark gaze. 'Eleanor would be better to stay indoors.'

'Oh, well.' Irene shrugged. 'If she prefers to she can always stay in her room and order a massage from one of their health professionals. I've read that some of those fellows are artists with their hands. I think she'd find it very therapeutic.'

Uncontrollably, Ellie's gaze flew to Sam's. The image flooded her brain of his smooth, bronzed hands as she'd known them on that night. Massaging her wild, willing body, with such masterly expertise. Kneading and caressing her breasts to erotic ecstasy. Exploring her satin secrets, his beautiful sexy mouth rousing her to rapture.

'She wouldn't,' he said, his voice as smooth as silk. 'You

wouldn't want some man coming to your room to rub you all over with essential oils, would you, Eleanor?'

Ellie was forced to lower her lashes. She felt an overwhelming rush of warmth to her breasts. 'I might,' she said, concealing her confusion behind an unfocused smile, her betraying voice overly husky. 'I'm not ruling anything out.' She felt his eyes on her hands, and saw they'd curled themselves up. Deliberately she made them unclench, and raised her gaze to his. His dark eyes were amused, but there was a hard sexual challenge in their depths that sent a fierce, responsive pang through her.

Irene gave a sigh of what sounded like contentment. She set down her cup and leaned her back against the sofa cushions. 'It's such a relief you're coming, Ellie. I had wanted Sam to come in the first place, but I think I'll have more fun with you. He never lets me have my head. I'll be able to try out the casino and the nightclubs, shop till I drop, do all the touristy things—'

Sam turned a thunderous gaze on his mother. 'I don't think so, Mum. You'll find it tiring enough just going to the wedding. Eleanor's job will be to keep you out of trouble.'

Irene looked solemn. 'I'll try to stay out of it, but you know how I am after champagne, dear. And knowing Jack and Rosemary, it'll be flowing from the moment we arrive.'

Ellie's lips twitched with the temptation to laugh, but she saw fatigue in Irene's face then, as if her store of energy for the day had suddenly been used up. Sam must have noticed it at the same time, because he got to his feet and ended the visit, with a peck on his mother's cheek and a quiet reminder to take her medication.

At the door Irene said, 'It's so kind of you to do this, Ellie. I hope Sam will be able to get along without you while you're away. But we won't be thinking about him, will we? We'll be too deeply immersed in the flesh pots of the Coast.'

Sam gave her an austere look and his lips thinned to a grim, straight line.

Ellie suppressed a laugh. She had to hand it to Irene. When it came to pressing buttons, she was a champ.

Sam was silent on the way down in the lift. He leaned against the wall, his hands in his pockets, his brooding dark gaze occasionally flicking to Ellie. When the doors opened on the ground floor the sound of a piano wafted their way. It was coming from the piano bar, set like an oasis in the vast lobby.

'I need a drink,' Sam said, taking her arm. 'This way, Ms O'Dea.'

The bar wasn't busy. The few customers chatting at nearby tables weren't audible above the notes dripping like honey from the fingers of the pianist. Ellie accepted the offer of a glass of red wine, and slid onto a bar-stool next to Sam's.

Her dress rode to mid-thigh, and she crossed her legs as the only possible safety measure. Sam swivelled his bar-stool round to face her, his dark-clad knee only centimetres from hers. 'You did very well then, Eleanor.' His gaze slid over her. 'My mother likes you.'

'I like her. She's funny.' She smiled at him, still cool, efficient Ms O'Dea on the surface, though her heart seemed to be in training for the Olympics.

'Funny, but deadly serious. She's a worry.'

She suffered one of those dangerous, weak melty moments she'd resolved to eliminate from her dealings with men. So he cared about his mother. Didn't they all?

She raised her wine to her lips. Sam continued to watch her while she took a tiny sip, his lashes half lowered. He murmured, 'Which queen was it whose skin was so transparent you could see the wine trickle down her throat?'

She met his shimmering dark gaze and felt her pulse hasten. 'Mary, Queen of Scots, I think. Though, you know, Sam, I suspect that story isn't true.'

'It might have been true, Eleanor,' he said gravely. 'If she was a Titian-haired beauty with skin like white satin.' He lapsed into a meditative silence while her head spun dizzily. Was this a compliment? Was he really saying that *she* was a…?

The wine radiated through her with a mellow warmth. It was so—pleasant being with him, not knowing what he might say next. She dangled on the edge of sweet suspense, waiting, in fact, *longing*, for him to make a move.

But he stared absently into his scotch. The bar's muted overhead light glanced off the chiselled planes and angles of his face from cheekbone to jaw. She had an overwhelming desire to touch his cheek and trace the lines with her fingers. Run her fingertips along that masculine mouth.

He held his glass loosely in his lean fingers, and gave the amber liquid an idle swirl, before connecting again with her eyes. 'It wouldn't be a good idea to let Mum do too much gallivanting, as she calls it.'

She nodded, uncrossing her legs. Funny how hard it was to keep four-inch heels on when perched on a bar-stool. Whichever way she disposed her legs, one of the shoes slipped halfway off to dangle, like some nightclub siren's. She wasn't intending to act seductively, but she couldn't help feeling it. It was the dress, and the look in his eyes whenever they lighted on her. She anchored one foot on the crossbar and let the other swing a little.

His heavy-lidded gaze scorched the length of her and back again. Her flesh rippled with fever, as if his lean, beautiful hands had actually touched her. Glances could burn, she mused, aware of that deep, sensual excitement she'd felt on the balcony at the masked ball. There could be the sensation of contact, even when people weren't touching.

His deep, dark voice seeped into her veins like an aphrodisiac. 'I'm depending on you to keep an eye on her.'

'Maybe you would be better to keep an eye on her yourself.'

He grimaced. 'No force on earth could get me to that wedding.' His gaze drifted to her mouth. 'All you have to do is to keep her from going overboard.'

'I'm sure she won't,' she rejoined, as steadily as possible for someone melting to the sexual pull of the most gorgeous man in Sydney. 'Irene doesn't strike me as someone who'd take unnecessary risks.'

His devil's eyebrows made a sardonic twitch. 'You don't know her. Once she gets with Aunt Rosemary there'll be no holding her.' He took a sip of his scotch. How could lashes so long and thick be so essentially masculine? 'It would be best if you could keep her in the suite.'

She roused herself from her voluptuous contemplation of him. 'In the suite!' she exclaimed. 'I'm going as her companion, not her gaoler.'

He put down his glass and leaned an arm along the bar, somehow enclosing her in a private little intimate enclave. Her heart made an adrenaline leap. If body language was anything to go by, Samos Stilakos was feeling very open towards her.

'Try to see it my way, Eleanor.' His deep velvet voice swayed her senses into a giddy hypnotic state. 'If you insist on all this sailing and carousing on the beach with strange men at midnight, how much of a companion are you likely to be?'

She gasped, and waved her glass in protest. 'I'm not insisting on anything!' A few drops of wine sloshed over the rim onto her fingers.

He took the glass from her hand and set it on the bar. Before she could reach for a paper serviette, he produced a beautifully laundered handkerchief, took her hand in his firm, light grip, and wiped her fingers with patient thoroughness.

'There, now.' He continued to hold her hand, and she held her breath. Desire coursed through her, sweet and irresistible as nectar. A piercing sensual gleam lit Sam's dark gaze, and for an electrified instant she thought he was going to raise her fingers to his lips. He said softly, 'We don't want to spoil that amazing dress. Not when you have to do dinner in it.'

Her voice came out as a husky croak. 'Dinner? Who said anything about dinner?'

He laughed and his deep, dark eyes lit with delight, and something like triumph. What had she said that was so funny?

And what did he have to feel triumphant about? She hadn't actually agreed to go to dinner, although there was no reason why she shouldn't. She was wearing a sexy, elegant dress, she was with a sophisticated man who made her feel desirable and interesting, and all she had planned for the evening was a comparative survey of the donor options offered by the various IVF clinics around the city.

She slid off the bar-stool and accompanied him out to where the car waited. Outside, she was surprised to see the first glimmerings of dusk. Lights seemed to be coming on all over the city. Somehow, in that wine bar, she'd lost all track of time.

Once in the car he gave his jaw a thoughtful rub. 'Er—do you mind coming home with me and waiting while I change, Eleanor?'

She looked quickly at him, but his expression was innocent. Nothing like that of a man set on whisking his PA to the nearest secluded venue, so he could ravish her into total delirium.

'Of course not.' She smiled, with her usual calm acceptance of anything a boss could throw at her.

CHAPTER FIVE

APARTMENT towers of steel and glass were hardly Ellie's style, but she couldn't deny the heady magnificence of Sam's sensational views across the city to the horizon. If he'd wanted to train a high-powered telescope on Hornsby, he'd probably be able to see the front door of her flat.

He parked her in his living area—although she wasn't sure who could ever live in such clean, uncluttered surroundings— while he vanished through an archway. The all-white room she was in disappeared around a corner into the unknown. It was all soaring ceilings, white marble surfaces and spiral staircases. He'd lived here for three years, he'd told her casually. Which meant post-Natalie.

Not the home of a man who wanted children in his life, was her first thought.

She wandered out onto the terrace, thankful for its high balustrade. Vertigo wasn't her favourite sensation. There was an inviting pool and spa, with lights glowing in their blue-green depths. A man attending to the Babylonian-style hanging gardens around the pool nodded to her, before gathering his equipment and disappearing inside.

If a man had all this, she reflected, a Porsche Carrera and a bank, what did he have left to strive for?

Around her the city was a-glitter as dusk gave way to dark.

Neon signs on neighbouring buildings pulsed with the same nervy rhythm the home territory of Samos Stilakos inspired in her heart.

However had she come to be in this place of all places? There was no way she should allow herself to succumb to another fling with him. Already she was struggling to maintain the barricades round her heart. She tried to remind herself of Mark's treachery, but found it hard to think of him here.

'It's too early in the evening for our balcony scene. You'd better come inside.'

The deep, mocking voice made her start. She turned and the breath seized in her throat. Sam stood at the terrace doors. He'd changed into casual trousers and a black, open-necked shirt. It deepened the velvet magnetism of his dark eyes and the olive tones in his skin, hung elegantly on his powerful frame, hinting at the muscled contours of his chest.

He looked relaxed and ready to play. Not the office Sam. The other one.

He strolled across to her. His hair was still damp from the shower, and he smelled of clean masculinity. He was her boss, she told herself giddily as an erotic mixture of tangy scents whooshed to her head.

Nothing was going to happen.

He reached out to touch her hair, further destabilising her. 'I can't wait to see you at the managers' meeting like this.' There was a glow in the depths of his dark eyes. 'I might have to make you do the presentation, so I can properly appreciate you from all angles.'

'Oh, but,' she replied, laughing, her pulse escalating, 'I can't just keep wearing this dress all the time. I've worn it today, and now tonight… It sounds as if you don't ever want me to take it off.'

He laughed wickedly and his arm snaked around her waist. 'Nothing could be further from the truth. Come inside and we'll talk about it.'

Inside the white room, a throaty female voice rendered a

sexy old jazz ballad with a moody mellowness. Candles had been lit, adding warmth to the room, and some antipasto and champagne had been laid out on a buffet cabinet. If this wasn't a scene set for seduction, her wires were seriously in need of straightening.

Sam opened the wine with casual expertise. 'I told my housekeeper how much you've eaten today, and she's worried.'

'What?' She cast a quick glance about. 'You mean—you have a woman here, on the premises?' Her words conjured instant visions of a Hollywood-style maid in a frilled apron, stilettos and nothing else, and as soon as they were out she went scarlet. 'Oh! I'm sorry, Sam!' *Dying* with embarrassment. If only she could sink through at least twenty-seven floors. 'Truly! I didn't mean that as it sounded.'

He surveyed her, amusement in his gaze, and handed her a glass. 'I do have a woman. Not exactly on the premises, but close to the premises. She lives a couple of floors below with her husband. That was Martin. You might have seen him outside earlier. He doubles as my driver.'

'Oh. Of course.' She gave a foolish laugh. 'What else?' She sank down onto a white sofa with her wine, and nearly lost her balance as the deep, decadent cushioning dragged her down into its sumptuous embrace. She saw Sam grin. What had happened to her legendary poise? Anyone would think she'd never been up in the stratosphere before with a sophisticated billionaire intent on having his way with her.

She laughed off her momentary disconcertion with graceful aplomb, but to be honest, faced with the old dilemma, her insides were churning. A massive risk was shaping up here. Her job, her plan, her foolish, stupid heart…

Looking too darkly sexy and nonchalant to be safe, Sam leaned against the buffet, sampling the occasional olive. He shot her a glance of lazy amusement. 'I'm sorry you find this room uncomfortable. If you like we can move somewhere else.' He tilted his dark head towards the archway.

What was through there? The master bedroom? 'No, no. It's not. It's—quite lovely here. Whatever makes you think I'm uncomfortable?'

'I've been studying your body language. I think I'm beginning to get the hang of it.'

A warning pang cut through her, but she saw the teasing light in his eyes and rose to the challenge, stretching her legs out in front of her and leaning back. 'You've got no chance,' she retorted with a careless laugh. 'I'm famous for my acting ability.'

'You're good, I admit that. *Yes, Mr Stilakos. No, Mr Stilakos*...as though we'd never been together.' He looked steadily at her and added softly, 'Never been lovers.'

Her heart made a wild leap and she quickly dropped her gaze, then, just as though his gleaming dark eyes weren't eating her up, and her pulse weren't madly racing, she said, 'What about you? You're very good yourself.' She put on a grim face and deepened her voice. 'So stern and dignified.'

His eyebrows twitched up in amusement. His gaze flickered to her legs, then met hers. 'Do you enjoy working?'

'Of course. I love it.'

'And you like the bank?'

She nodded.

'You've been there a long time,' he observed lazily. 'Have you ever considered exploring further afield?'

She shrugged. 'Not really. I've liked all the jobs I've had there.'

He picked up a small platter of the antipasto and strolled across to her with it. 'And you're very talented. Always cool, never ruffled. Always smiling and pleasant. Beautiful, efficient Ms O'Dea. But what goes on underneath?' He dropped down beside her and offered her the food. 'Who was the guy who taught you to play it safe?' His tone was casual, but no way was this a casual question, and his eyes pierced her with an alertness that threatened to penetrate her crucial internal fortifications. 'What do you think about when the lights go out, Eleanor?'

'Nothing.' She smiled and fluttered her lashes. 'You keep me working so hard, I just fall straight to sleep when the lights go out.' She accepted a caviare-laden cracker with the same calm smile, and forced herself to bite into it. But it was damnably hard to swallow. Her heart had started an uncomfortable pounding, and he was close. Far too close. This was hardly the seduction line she'd expected.

His long muscled leg was near enough to brush hers and light her up with fireworks. One part of her wanted it to happen, but another part wanted to run to the balcony and jump on the first passing jet to Hornsby. Was it fair for a boss to delve into the private personal heart of his PA?

Her aching cheeks needed a rest. She got off the sofa and strolled about, pretending to study the art works with interest, as conscious of the current between them as if it were tangible. In need of a breathing space, she stopped in front of a square of white canvas.

'What do you think?' he said, coming to stand next to her. The black hairs on his forearm lightly grazed her arm, with electric results. 'Inspiring? Uplifting?'

She put her head on one side as coolly as if her awareness of him weren't pulsing through her veins. The skin where his arm had brushed hers instantly craved it again, and she couldn't resist swaying imperceptibly closer for another touch. 'It's white,' she said, fleetingly closing her eyes to savour the brief tingling contact. 'Certainly a clean look.'

'Not empty and lifeless, like this place?'

'Don't you like it here?' She glanced wonderingly around at all the trappings of understated luxury that could only be available to the very, very rich, and risked turning to look at him.

His sensual dark gaze riveted her to the floor. 'I think I like it better this evening than I ever have before.' There was no easy smile with the words. His gorgeous, sexy mouth was as grave as if he were speaking from the heart.

With masterful ease he caught her in his arms. The dark desire in his eyes seared her like a flame. She'd play it cool this time, her wild thoughts flew. Hold back. Try not to expose herself as a weak, vulnerable fool.

But he held her head between his hands and kissed her, and her susceptible body surged to his remembered touch in rapturous welcome.

There was no playing it cool. At the first brush of his lips desire blazed in her blood like a bushfire. Just as he had the first time, he tasted her mouth with a tenderness so ravishing it turned her knees to water, and her breasts swelled in arousal as he slid his teeth across her lower lip with slow, sexy eroticism.

He pulled her hard into him and deepened the kiss, intensifying the intimacy by slipping his tongue inside and plundering her mouth with an artful teasing she was powerless to resist.

Helpless thrills quivered through her as his long fingers stroked the length of her spine and moulded her to his hard, vibrant body. She clung to him, her bones melting, a sweet urgency between her thighs, her breasts and straining nipples in delicious friction with his chest.

She kneaded his powerful shoulders and gave herself up to the voluptuous pleasure of his big, lean frame in contact with her soft curves. The taste and scent of him fuelled her potent memories of him, and fanned the flames of her secret longings.

He snatched the very air from her lungs. The kiss deepened to a molten pitch, her passion for more of him fighting with her need for oxygen. But he was in supreme control. In the very nick of time his sensual hands traversed her arms to her shoulders, and he ended it, breaking from her.

She swayed a little on her four-inch heels, light-headed for lack of oxygen, and he put a hand on her shoulder. 'Steady there,' he said with some amusement. But for all his cool, his deep voice sounded dark and gravelly, and through his dark lashes his eyes were black fire. 'That's how I remembered you tasting,' he said, exultation in his voice.

Knowing she was flushed and dishevelled, she angled away from him and made an effort to tidy her hair and smooth down her dress. 'How?' she said croakily, panting, shocked by the un-controlled response he'd raised in her. With just a kiss!

'Sexy. Sweet. *Wild.*'

His eyes were smouldering, and her heart trembled at the in-tensity betrayed by his voice. Summoned by his mesmeric gaze, she felt overwhelmingly tempted to throw caution to the winds and melt back into his arms. Dimly her mind grappled with the awesome strength of the passion threatening to unleash itself in her. Had it always been there, or was it only when *he* touched her?

'I've thought of you so often since that night, dream girl,' he said thickly, reaching to twine a strand of her hair behind her ear. 'I've never met a woman like you.'

Dream girl! *Her?* But he was Samos Stilakos, and she was just… If he knew even the half of her ordinary old reality! No one had ever said anything so romantic to her, and, though he sounded sincere, how could he be believed? It was all happening too fast.

Unsure of how to respond, she backed a little away from him. 'Isn't it time for us to leave? For—for the restaurant?'

He blinked, but before he could make another move she excused herself as gracefully as she could, considering the strained breathlessness of her voice, swooped on her bag, and escaped to the guest bathroom.

Safe inside, she leaned back against the door and closed her eyes. *Dream girl.* The question had to be faced. Had he given her the job because she'd slept with him? And…because he wanted a repeat performance of that night? But he would have to remember her absolute rejection of an affair. He must.

Perhaps, though… An excitement there was no repressing uncoiled inside her. If there was a chance he was sincere, if that night was still as vivid to him as it was to her…

If he'd truly felt that deep connection, and craved *more*…

She hugged her arms tightly around her. There were reasons she mustn't succumb, she knew, but she needed time to recall them. Just a little time.

After a few moments of deep breathing, she recovered some semblance of sanity and came to a decision. If he did expect more she would have to remind him of her unshakeable stance on affairs, leave with stylish dignity and go straight home. Otherwise…well, otherwise, she'd just go with the flow and… go with the flow.

She washed and applied fresh make-up, and smeared her lips with moisturiser.

When she emerged Sam had slipped on a jacket, and held the car keys dangling from his lean fingers. The glance he gave her from beneath his dark brows was searching.

'Everything all right?' he enquired.

She smiled and arched her brows. 'Of course. Everything's fine.'

They didn't have far to drive to The Rocks. He parked the car in one of the small, private car parks converted from the old cellars of some adjoining buildings in the wharf area. As they climbed the stairs to the street he put a hand on her elbow to steady her, almost as a lover would, or a husband.

The restaurant he'd chosen was famous for its cuisine and glittering clientele. She made a covert survey of the room for famous faces, only to find numerous heads swivelling *their* way.

Their table was discreetly placed, perfect for a lover's tryst, or a quiet interrogation between boss and PA. 'Every man in this room envies me,' Sam murmured, with a gentle but possessive touch in the small of her back as the *maître d'* pulled out her chair.

She looked enquiringly at him, and her heart trembled at the warmth in his dark glance. 'Do you sweet-talk all your PAs so outrageously when you wine them and dine them?' she said, once they were settled and he'd ordered the wine.

Amusement glimmered in his eyes. 'I don't wine them and dine them.'

Questions clamoured in her brain. The evidence pointed another way. She needed to get things straight. Was she dining with him as a woman, or as his PA?' 'But here you are,' she persevered, 'wining and dining *me*, sweet-talking me—'

'*Kissing* you.' His eyes darkened and he leaned forward, making her gasp as he traced her lower lip with a sensual fingertip. The bold desire in his eyes threatened to send her insides into meltdown all over again. 'How else am I to get to know you?'

Her heart bounded in her chest. Could she be hearing aright? Wasn't this the theme of her most extreme fantasy?

He sat back, a small frown creasing his brow. 'I know what's worrying you. It's tricky when office rules get tangled up with a genuine attraction. The important thing is not to let it get in the way.'

Her breath caught. 'The—the attraction?'

'No. The office.'

The words sank in. Samos Stilakos, worldly, sophisticated, gorgeous and elusive target for equally sophisticated, beautiful women, was spelling it out. To *her*.

'Do you believe in magic?' His warm, ardent gaze thrilled her. 'It might sound like a cliché, but what else can you call it when you meet someone—in the unlikeliest circumstances!—and instantly feel that rare connection?'

The breath caught in her throat. Hadn't this been her own instinct at their first encounter?

'What do you think?' he added, seduction in his dark eyes, in the smile playing on his sensuous mouth. 'Am I telling it like it is? Do you feel it too?'

Her lashes fluttered uncontrollably, much like her unsafe heart. Sweet talk had rarely been more convincing, or exciting. 'I think you're giving me the rush,' she said huskily, almost needing to cling to the table edge. 'I think you're making my head spin.'

'I hope so, Eleanor. I hope your head's spinning. You're not convincing me with that oh, so cool and collected act. Not when I know how hot the little siren is who's hiding behind that face.'

Visions rose in her mind of some of her unprecedented, adventurous acts of passion on the Night of Nights, and she couldn't prevent a fiery blush from rising up from her toes and infusing her entire body.

He grinned, as if the scorching scenes flashing through her mind were just as visible to him. Impossibly, she felt her blush deepen. In an attempt to cool her confusion she reached for her wine, took a much larger gulp than was wise and nearly choked.

Sam laughed and his lashes descended in satisfaction. 'Paydirt! Come on, then. I want to know everything about you. If you could have anything you wanted in the world, what would be your deepest, most fervent desire?'

She gazed at his lean, handsome face, smiling at her with such challenging warmth, and the truth resonated in her heart with a certainty that shook her to her soul.

Her chance to have a child, that was certain, but was that all? Didn't she want it the easy way? The old-fashioned, loving way? With someone she loved, who could love her?

Someone like…?

Her mind reared back from the unthinkable. Her lips parted, but no words came.

All her flippant protestations at Beth's warnings flashed before her now for the hollow bravado they had been. Who had she been kidding? She hadn't just taken the job for the money. She'd wanted to be close to him. How foolish and predictable. If she didn't fight it, the same old dreams would drive her to heartbreak now as inexorably as they had in the past. The next thing she knew, she'd be giving in to imagining floating down the aisle, visualising nights in the arms of her loving husband, dreaming of his beautiful, dark-eyed children…

'All right, let me guess,' he said. 'You'll never be happy until you're CEO of the bank. You want my job.' He spoke lightly, but all at once the question in his gaze was serious.

But if there was one certain thing her advanced years had taught her, it was how fast he'd vanish in a puff of smoke if she revealed the naked truth. So she deflected the query with an easy laugh. 'You're so right, Sam. How did you guess? And—and what would be your most fervent desire?'

His eyes veiled, and he lowered his black lashes. 'Ah… well…ordinary things. It's amazing how hard they are to come by, though, isn't it? You think you have them in your grasp, and then…' He shrugged and drained his glass.

What couldn't he come by easily? she wondered. A man as blessed as he'd been, with wealth, charm, genuine masculine beauty… Was he referring to Natalie?

'I often think now it would be good to live on an island,' he continued, 'without all the chaos, where life was simple.' He shrugged. 'There, that's probably my genes talking. My grandfather hailed from Samos, in the Aegean.' His eyes smiled into hers, and he reached across the table for her hand. 'I'll take you there one day, Eleanor, and show you.'

Such a beautiful promise. How many women had he made it to? But it enchanted her all the way down to her curled-up toes.

He told her other things, about his boyhood, his father, the mischief he and his cousin had got up to together. His words evoked a world of family life and good times, of beaches and bush picnics, far removed from the world he inhabited now. Despite her turmoil, she felt herself falling deeper under his spell. If only he wouldn't grin in that seriously weakening way. It was too easy to visualise the boy he must have been—the sweet, sexy, macho boy.

Perhaps she could risk one more time. Mightn't it be possible to have one more fling with him? One last fantastic night?

The waiter brought their meals, but she hardly noticed the food. She was too heavily in thrall to the most charming seducer in Sydney. But though he flattered her with his wicked words, there was sincerity in his gaze too, and warmth in his smile. His velvet eyes dwelled on her as if she were the most interesting and desirable woman in the world. She found herself telling him things about her life and her friends as if *he* were a friend. He flirted with her, mocked her and made her laugh, just as he had on that night.

All the time, though, it was clear where it was heading. The knowledge was in his every glance, in every brush of his fingers.

When they were offered the dessert menu, he said, 'Shall we stay here for dessert, or head somewhere else?' His mouth was grave, but the shimmer in his dark eyes was the colour of sin.

When had she ever resisted dessert?

CHAPTER SIX

WAS he drunk, Sam wondered, or was it the summer night that made him want to leap and spin about in some crazy dance? Strolling the uneven streets beside Ellie O'Dea, he pretended to catch his shoe, and lingered back a step to drink in the radiance of her heavy fall of hair, the subtle sway of her taut little edible behind.

The image of her moonlit shape on the hotel balcony rushed back to him with its erotic power, and his blood stirred with the old enchantment. She cast him back an enquiring smile, a sparkle in her eyes as if she guessed his small subterfuge. He grinned and caught her up again. The chemistry was magic, he thought with escalating excitement, but still he sensed a tension in her, a restraint.

How did she manage to remain so elusive? He could gaze into those clear, smiling eyes till he drowned, but why did it feel as if she were still wearing her mask? Since the first, every step he took with her was a tread on eggshells. Any false move, and she might vanish into the night as easily as she'd slipped through his fingers on that fateful dawn.

They reached the entrance to the car park and he used his security key to unlock the street door. Despite their renovation, the fishy harbour smell still permeated the dank walls of the old cellars, and rose to greet him as they descended to the lower floor.

The few other cars parked there earlier had departed, and only the Porsche remained. Their steps echoed in the empty place.

They reached the shadowy alcove where the car was parked, and stopped to face each other. In the sudden silence and isolation, Sam felt an urgency to break through the constraints. They'd been lovers once. They would be again. Why pretend?

He scanned her face and said, his voice catching with the force of his desire, 'Do you know how much I want you?'

In the shadowy light uncertainty swirled in her eyes as she searched his face. After a heartbeat's hesitation she said, 'No—yes. Perhaps.'

'Do you ever tell the truth?' In mock frustration, he wound a swathe of her hair around his hand, held it to his face and inhaled its honeyed scent. The intoxication of it, the memories it evoked, flooded him with lust, and he groaned. In his urgent need to pin her down he took her smooth, satin arms in his hands. 'You do know. We both know. Tell the truth. You haven't forgotten what it was like that night! You still want me!'

His passionate conviction swept Ellie along on a giddy, irresistible tide. With her pulse thundering in her ears, she confessed tremulously, 'No, Sam, I haven't forgotten. I want you.'

He held her a little closer. His deep voice, his dark eyes, were compelling. 'And we'll always be honest with each other. Lovers without lies. Do you agree?'

Lovers. On his tongue the word had such thrilling connotations she felt as if she'd been transported to some magic realm where everything was possible. Hope shivered down her spine.

'Hey.' Concern shone in his eyes. 'You're cold.' He slipped off his jacket and hung it around her shoulders.

The moment was so reminiscent of that first night, she was overwhelmed with the strongest sensation of *déjà vu*. He stood surveying her in it, his eyes growing more darkly intense and smoulderingly sexual, and her stomach coiled in excitement.

He pulled her against him and kissed her with hungry passion. His insistent lips demanded her equal response, and she surrendered to the sizzling assault and gave in, kissing him back with fervour as the ready fire ignited in her blood.

Her knees weakened, and she raised her arms around his neck, clutching at his thick black hair, heedless of the damp pungent smells of harbour and wet cement in the old converted cellar.

The element of risk in their dark corner reminded her of the forbidden flavour of their first embrace. She remembered how they'd urged each other on to greater and greater acts of abandonment, and it induced her to throw caution to the winds. She wanted him to do more than kiss her, and he seemed to know it.

He pushed her back against the car, his mouth on her throat and collar-bone, his lean, bronzed hands caressing her swollen breasts, seeking the taut nipples, inflaming them through her clothes.

He lowered his dark head, and through the light fabric took first one, then the other sensitive peak in his mouth to suck and tease. It brought her to such an intense pitch of wild, sweet pleasure that her desire roared through her like a firestorm and flamed between her thighs.

But their clothes were in the way. With feverish hands she tore at his shirt buttons and revealed his powerful, bronzed chest. Then, with hands and mouth, she explored the rippling satin skin with its whorls of black hair. She felt his flat nipples tauten under her tongue, relishing her power to send pleasure shuddering through his big, strong frame.

Panting, she stood back to enjoy the sight of him in disarray, his gorgeous chest gleaming from his open shirt, his breath tearing and catching like hers, his eyes dark and heavy-lidded in arousal.

She wanted more.

Instinctively, as though attuned to her hunger, he pushed up her dress and laid her thighs bare. 'Such charming thighs,' he murmured, his voice gravelled, eyes black as Lucifer's.

She waited, panting, for his next move. She felt as if she were on fire, her body a vessel of desire, his every light touch a match to the flame of her overheated flesh. He placed a caressing hand on her knee, then, with tantalising slowness, traced a wicked, purposeful finger up her leg, slipping it inside her inner thigh to tease the silken, sensitive skin there. With charged fingers he stroked closer, and ever deliciously closer, to the hot, urgent place concealed by her flimsy little panties.

She dug her fingers into his powerful shoulders, and held her breath, her heart's blood thundering in her ears, aching, aching for him to go the whole way. At the elastic's edge, his caressing hand paused for an electric, tingling instant, then, when suspense brought her nearly to breaking-point, crept on, to traverse the fabric across her vibrant mound. She clung to him, unbreathing, hypnotised by the dark magic of his touch.

He slipped his fingers underneath the fabric, and she quivered and gasped in delight. With sensual, knowing strokes he parted her sensitive folds while she leaned back against the car, half clinging to him in swooning ecstasy, on fire for him to find the pulsating pleasure spot at the centre. He made contact and she gave a small, wrenching cry. Tenderly, expertly he caressed her throbbing clitoris, then slipped a finger inside her slick, moist channel and stroked, rousing her with astonishing speed to a sweet, sobbing climax.

She sagged against him, supported in his arms, her face buried in his strong neck. He held her there for some heart-thundering moments, then tilted her back and brushed her face with quick little tender kisses. After a few seconds he let her go, and they contemplated each other in the pulsing silence.

Her heart thudded. Challenge gleamed in his fierily aroused eyes. Instinctively she understood the question. How far did she dare to go with him? In tacit response she ran her tongue-tip over her dry lips, then gasped with shock as in a quick, wicked movement he whipped down her pants.

His audacity exhilarated her. The element of danger pushed her passion and excitement to an even wilder pitch. Spurred to respond, she grasped his belt buckle and released it, and heard his sharp intake of breath as she slid her hand down to caress the promising virile bulge inside his trousers.

'Quickly, quickly,' she panted, and tried to help him to ease the zip down over his erection.

He gave a strangled laugh, and pushed her hands away to free himself unaided. With wide-eyed anticipation, she surveyed his impressive arousal, rock-hard and rampant. He swept her onto his lap as he lowered himself onto the car's bonnet, and, with swift efficiency, positioned her so she was face to face with him.

She gave a sensual little wriggle, then levered herself to ease down on him, gasping with delight as his velvet hardness filled her. Then, holding her tight in his arms, his chest grazing her breasts, he rocked her, gazing into her eyes as he thrust repeatedly into her. In an escalating rhythm, he stroked her inner flesh, completely filling her sheath with such delicious, heavenly vigour, she could only cry out with each amazing plunge.

The sweetness and intensity of being held and gazed at and rocked with such thrilling intimacy rushed her up a wild, steep curve of gasping excitement, to an explosive, rippling climax.

After the last rapturous aftershock they stilled, gazes meshed in a primitive communion. At last the distant sound of voices from the street jolted them from their pleasure. Sam eased her onto her feet. Shakily, she scrambled to tidy her clothes, while he refastened his.

He stared at her, his breathing ragged as he surveyed her panting dishevelment. 'Let's go home,' he murmured, and opened the car door and ushered her inside.

He settled in beside her and bent to softly kiss her mouth. When he drew back she touched his face. She felt wrapped in a cocoon of blissful accord with him, knowing she was able to match his need for passion and excitement, as he matched hers.

'Not the place I would have chosen,' he murmured in his deep voice, his hand possessive on her thigh. 'We'll do better next time. Where do you live?'

'Hornsby.'

'Hornsby! My God,' he groaned, then fired the engine. After

he nosed the car out into the street, he gave her an intense, glowing look. 'Has anyone ever told you what a beautiful and exciting, *sensual* woman you are?'

'You did,' she answered huskily. 'On the night of the masked ball.' He laughed a husky laugh, and, secure in the warmth of his admiration, she stayed enveloped in her dreamy, magical cocoon all the way to Hornsby.

It wasn't so far, now the night-time traffic had diminished a little. After a while her breathing calmed and she fell silent. The silence pulsed with the anticipation of more passion to come.

Sam occasionally glanced her way to make some observation, but she was barely aware of the Sydney nightscape. She was thinking about what would happen next. About making love with him again. In her bed.

Samos Stilakos. In her bedroom.

She made a mental review of the room, trying to visualise him in it. She hoped she'd made her bed. After the luxury of his sky-palace she wondered what he would think of rugs picked up cheap from the Taj Bazaar, and cushions embroidered by her mother's tapestry circle. It was hard to imagine him in her flat. She had the unpleasant realisation that it would declare, far more stridently than words ever could, the inequalities between the Boss and his PA.

What if one of her friends drove by and saw the Porsche? How would it look to them? The romantic cloud she was floating on lost a bit of height. A nasty little voice from her daily down-to-earth self piped up. What had he actually said to her that meant anything? Had she just allowed herself to be carried away?

'You'd better direct me from here,' he said in his deep, quiet voice.

She started, realising how close they were, and with a racing pulse gave him some directions that brought them into the entrance of her street. 'Along here, on the left.' She almost wished she could tell him to turn around and go in the opposite direction.

She swallowed. 'That's it there. The duplex.'

Her heart seized then as she was struck by the most horrible thought.

Hadn't she left all that stuff she'd downloaded about the IVF process on the kitchen table? *And* there were coloured brochures from the clinics.

She blenched at the thought of him seeing them. How much would it reveal about her? Her failure to find a partner in time. Her *desperation…*? A man with his razor-sharp intelligence would put two and two together and comprehend it all.

Perspiration broke out on her upper lip. She couldn't invite him in.

She dug her fingers into her palms. It would be too much to hope he'd had enough loving for one night. Even if he didn't want to make love again, he'd expect her to ask him in for coffee.

Her heart began to thump with the most ridiculous, erratic rhythm, and she uncurled her hands and surreptitiously put them to her cheeks. What had she done? She'd asked for this. She'd got herself into it, and now there was no graceful way out.

He drew up under the streetlamp in front of her gate and turned off the engine. The silence grew electric. She sat taut and still in her seat, tension gripping her throat. He turned his head to examine her with a questioning gaze. She knew what he expected.

What she'd led him to expect.

He thought she would take him through her front door, lead him to her bedroom, take him into her bed. Or at least show him into her kitchen and sit him down at the table, with a coffee mug filled with instant.

He smiled and touched her cheek, his dark eyes warm. 'Is coffee on offer?'

Her eyelids lowered. How could she refuse? 'Of course.' She forced a smile.

His brows twitched curiously as he studied her face, but he sprang out and swiftly came around to open her door. She got out, and, with his arm around her, walked through the gate and up the path with him, every step a step closer to mortification, her brain teeming with desperate measures.

She would have to make him promise on his honour not to read anything. Or he'd have to promise not to go into the kitchen. But what if she'd left the literature on her bedside table? That was a real possibility. If she had, what were the chances he'd be able to avoid it?

There was only one solution.

No way, *no way* could she let him in, and she would have to find a compelling reason.

They arrived at her front door, and the security lamp switched itself on. She delved into her bag for the keys, but her shaking hands were ineffectual. After a hectic few moments, Sam took the bag from her hands, held it to his ear and gave it a shake. He plunged his hand in, and with a couple of deft movements produced the keys. 'Is this them?'

She nodded.

He handed them to her, murmuring, 'One of the few worthwhile things a man derives from a marriage. The ability to find a woman's keys.'

She slipped the key into the lock, then turned to face him, her back to the door. She cleared her throat. 'Look. About the coffee, Sam—' Her voice was embarrassingly strained.

He searched her face. 'You're out of coffee?' He smiled, desire smouldering in his eyes. 'What is it? You don't want to invite me in, is that it?'

She'd thought of a reason. Still, her heart pounded like a coward's to use it. 'I can't,' she said. 'Not—not tonight. Not like this.'

'Like what?'

She made an inarticulate gesture. 'Like—the way we are.'

His dark gaze scanned her face. 'How are we?'

'I like you very much, of course—'

He laughed, but his eyes were watchful. 'I'd hope so, after what just happened.'

She flushed, intensely conscious of her wanton compliance a bare half-hour before. 'Yes, yes, I know, but—' she steeled herself '—you're my boss.'

The silence missed a heavy beat. 'So?'

With trepidation she realised that a rejection now would go hard, but anything was better than risking him seeing those brochures. She took a deep breath, and asserted with only a slight tremor in her voice, 'I work for you. It's not exactly a free and open relationship, is it?'

Somewhere underneath her bravado her heart was still madly thumping. She studied him suspensefully, her hands clenched.

He shook his head and blinked in disbelief. 'Let me get this straight. You're bringing *this* down to office politics?'

The stunned question in his eyes, and the tone of his voice, made it sound as if he believed that what was happening between them was something very special and romantic. She was swayed with sudden doubt. There had been those moments, compelling moments, when she'd believed in his sincerity, those tiny glimpses into his real self.

Shame threatened her certainty. The word *betrayal* popped into her head.

'Oh, well,' she faltered confusedly, 'isn't it a matter of ethics?'

Samos Stilakos made a searing intake of breath. His eyebrows shot up and he stared at her. 'What? You're telling *me* about—?' He straightened up to his full height and reeled back a step, as if his very honour had suffered a mortal wound. His eyes turned to jet. For an instant his strong, handsome face was frozen in outrage.

Then he met her paralysed gaze and made a visible effort to recover his control.

Guilt began to flood through her, but after a few heart-stopping seconds he merely shook his head and shrugged. If he was enraged at such an insult, he summoned formidable restraint to conceal it.

Why did he have to be such a gentleman? It made her excuse all the weaker.

'So it's goodnight, then,' he said, back to being polite after the warmth and intimacy of the evening. He searched her face with a frown, then shrugged again and turned away from her, his eyes as chill and remote as the polar icecap.

She felt punished. It was as if the sun had gone out. Irrationally then, she wished he could at least kiss her good-night. 'I'm sorry, Sam,' she said nervously before he could walk down the path and leave her alone. 'No hard feelings. Won't you at least—shake hands?'

He turned. The glance he shot her from beneath his sardonic brows pierced her as if she were transparent, right through to her marshmallow spine. It was deeply discomfiting. 'Would this be about the *adventurer*, by any chance?' he said drily.

She gasped, momentarily struck speechless, and shook her head in utter, absolute rejection. 'Wh-what?' she stuttered. 'What are you talking about! No! As if *he*— As if *that*—' She took a deep breath. '*That* has nothing to do with *this*.' Anger made her unusually reckless, and she started to talk very rapidly, her words nearly falling over each other in her need to defend herself. 'If you must know I'm wondering about the others,' she blustered, with a defiant glare. 'You know— Schanelle, Vanessa, Sasha…' She waved her hand about agitatedly to indicate the dozens, probably thousands of women he'd seduced and forgotten, but when she saw his expression her heart shuddered to a halt. 'Everyone knows what happened with them,' she squeezed out.

His eyes had turned as hard as stone, his mouth a grim, straight line. She felt more than a bit frightened. For once she'd really lost her cool.

He said in a clipped, level voice, 'Sasha left because her fiancé was transferred to Brisbane. Schanelle got a better job offer in the Prime Minister's department in Canberra. Vanessa lost her position because she'd falsified her qualifications and wasn't up to the job.'

'Oh.' There was no mistaking the authority of the words. She sagged back against the door, aghast at the fool she'd made of herself. 'Oh. Oh, I'm sorry. I shouldn't have said— Sam…'

'Forget it,' he said coldly. 'You were right. *This* would be wrong. My mistake, Ms O'Dea. I apologise for harassing you.' He swung sharply on his heel and walked away.

She didn't watch him leave. She turned her face to the door. As her key turned in the lock she heard the gate click shut. It cut through her with a lonely, final sound.

She nearly fell into the hall, tripping over a pile of rubbish just inside the door. She kicked it aside and hit the light switch. Numbly, she stumbled to the kitchen.

A jumble of indigestible emotions seized her, so intense she could have screamed. She noticed the muddle of papers and booklets scattered across the table, and swiped them to the floor. Then she thought better of it, picked them up, tore them into frantic little pieces and thrust them into the bin.

This was the time for alcohol. But she never kept the stuff in her flat, and had to resort to warming milk in the microwave. She drank a few sips, then made for the shower, taking care not to look at herself in any mirror along the way.

She felt as if something huge and jagged had lodged in her chest. It wasn't until she emerged from the bathroom clean, scrubbed and pyjamaed, her hair in a pony-tail, prepared for a final check of the locks, that she noticed the rubbish in the hall.

It had been a pile of bags and boxes delivered by courier, no doubt neatly stacked inside by her kindly next-door neighbour, who must have used the emergency key she held. Now it was a dishevelled mess, boxes with their lids off, tissue-swathed fabrics spilling out, shoes she could never have afforded, skewed across the floor.

She recognised them all, of course. They were the other things she'd tried on today that she'd liked. They amounted to a fortune's worth. How could a man so concerned with the bank's bottom line be so generous?

Then with sudden anger she thought, how dared he do this?

How dared he not accept her refusal? What sort of man could not take *no* for an answer?

Long into the restless night, as she tossed in her empty bed her brain churned with the answers. *Arrogant, domineering, controlling, underhanded, cunning…*

She kept remembering that humiliating moment when he'd looked at her as if he could see right through to her very soul. The sheer, infuriating gall of it.

What could a man like *him* know about a woman like *her*?

CHAPTER SEVEN

SAM groaned and rolled over.

A minute later he was on his feet, dragging on gym shoes, shorts and singlet. A brisk run through the dawn streets of the old city was often the most pleasant start to the day, but not this day. This day required a punishing routine in the basement gym, followed by a stiff workout in the pool.

By the time he'd showered and shaved, donned an impeccably laundered shirt and tied his silk tie, he'd worked out a sane approach. He'd tell her succinctly that any personal association between them was in the past. He'd make it clear he had a bank to run and would not tolerate the distractions of feminine behaviour. He'd offer her a transfer...

Though what if she took it up?

No. He doubted she would. Where would she find conditions to equal what she had?

But as for the *personal* front...

In the Sirius basement he used his pass-key for the lift. As the lift drew closer to his floor the recollection of her astounding behaviour grew sharper and more stinging. Ellie O'Dea would learn he was not a man desperate for the company of beautiful women. The world was awash with redheads more beautiful.

More honest. More open, more straightforward.

More receptive. More compliant.

More *grateful* to have been offered the opportunity of

enjoying an entire night with a virile and sensitive lover. If she only knew the desperate lengths some women had gone to to catch his eye. Actresses. *Models.*

Contrary to what he'd expected, and had carefully primed himself for, she wasn't at her desk, and there was no sign of her having arrived and gone off somewhere.

He frowned. Excellent. That gave him more time to concentrate on the important matters of the day. Although... She wouldn't have taken the day off, would she? Or...

A paralysing thought struck him. What if she'd decided against coming back at all?

Ellie woke late. She knew Sam would have been expecting her to be there before him, but after the heavy night she found it impossible to hurry.

Her hair took ages to dry, it wouldn't twirl neatly into its roll, and in the end, in desperation, she left it down. When it came to dressing she remembered that her better business suit was in Sam's car and the other at the cleaner's.

It was an emergency. She had her pride to consider. A woman in her situation couldn't, just couldn't, face the man again in nasty old clothes. There was only one thing for it.

On the way in to work she took a detour.

At David Jones it was early in the shoppers' day, and there were few others to contend with. Knowing instinctively this was not a battle that could be won with inferior weapons, she bypassed the floor of cheaper brands to head straight for the designer section.

Driven by the clock, she had to make her choice quickly. The first thing that called to her was a slim black dress. It was chic and feminine, with small cap sleeves in black embroidered tulle, and a price tag she'd have gasped at only a day earlier. With her rich red hair and white skin it looked stunning. She agonised over it for several uncertain minutes. No one had ever shown up at work in such a dress. She'd have to adjust her IVF timeline. Was a job worth so much sacrifice?

Yes! The answer rang in her head like a bell.

The saleswoman looked doubtful when Ellie said she'd prefer to keep it on and wear it to work, but she'd made her decision. It made a hole in her savings account, but she paid for it with barely a flinch.

It was only when she left the shop that she allowed herself to acknowledge the knot in her chest connected with Sam. Every step closer to the bank was an ordeal, but if she could just get past this one difficult day with him…

By the time she arrived the building was humming. People she passed stared and said, 'Ellie! *Amazing* dress,' and she smiled as though it were a normal day and everything was fine. Not that she was nervous. Not exactly. He would be as courteous as ever, she felt sure. That was the hard thing about him. He could be polite and freeze people to death, even when he wasn't sacking them.

It was past ten when she stepped out on her floor. Almost time for his coffee. She dropped her bag beside her desk, and hurried to put the milk she'd bought in the fridge.

Inside, at his executive rosewood desk, Sam heard the sounds of arrival. He tensed, and glanced at his desk-clock with narrowed eyes.

Let her explain *this*.

He rose, adjusted belt and tie, and strolled to the door with the commanding, panther-like stride of Company Director and Chief Executive Officer.

She had her back to him, organising the espresso machine. Straight away he noticed she had her hair out again, hanging like a rich, silken waterfall. At the sound of the opening door she turned, and his insides were blown away.

Black. The dress was black. And above the lacy bodice the hint of her breasts glowed pearlescent white, like satin. And her legs. Her endless, endless legs. And surely her mouth was fuller and riper after last night's kissing? And her eyes, glittering like some— Dammit, he had to get a grip. Hadn't he learned? That glittering quality meant she was calculating something.

He said brusquely, 'You're late.'

Ellie heard the accusation in his tone and flushed. 'I know. I'm sorry. I was held up.' She saw his mouth thin, and hastened to placate him. 'I— Would you like some coffee?'

His expression froze. She realised the ghastliness of what she'd said and her heart plunged. For a horrified moment she hung there speechless, then pulled herself together to say faintly, 'Are you ready for—?'

He cut her off with a cool rejoinder. 'I've had coffee, thanks. Have you remembered the managers' meeting at ten-thirty?'

'Yes. Yes, of course.'

Damn. She'd forgotten it, but she still had ten minutes left in which to set up the boardroom. She'd already prepared illustrated take-home booklets for the managers, to support the presentation she'd helped Sam put together. At least she had no need to be ashamed of her work. She'd put a lot into it, and the booklet was a classy little production.

Sam strode away, and Ellie hurried to the boardroom. She placed the stack of booklets in a safe place for distribution at the end of the meeting, while she checked the audio-vis equipment, and set out the requisite stationery and mineral water on the oval table.

The managers began to trickle in, most of them greeting her with the easy familiarity of long acquaintance.

'What's this about a crèche in the building?'

With a jolt of alarm, Ellie saw that Trevor from Sales had spotted the booklets she'd prepared, and taken one to his place. 'Don't tell me we're doing an about-face and changing into a sensitive New Age bank,' he complained, idly flicking through it.

She was about to dive over and snatch it off him when Margot from Product Assessments, who still wore big eighties hair, leaned over to squint at it. 'Where'd you get this?' She perused the page, raising her Elizabeth Taylor eyebrows. 'Show me where it mentions the crèche.'

The manager on Trevor's left wanted to see as well, and in

a short space of time several of them were loudly debating the pros and cons of having a childcare facility on the premises.

Ellie watched in apprehension, fearful of Sam arriving while they were talking about it. At any other time she'd have been delighted by their interest. She'd had a vague hope that, by including the research she'd gathered so the managers could take it away with them, the idea of a bank-funded nursery to support working mothers might grow, and have a trickle-up effect. It had been a momentary impulse to slip the page in. She'd half intended to slip it out again before the meeting, but yesterday's tumultuous events had completely wiped it from her mind.

The trouble was, Sam hadn't exactly approved her initiative. In fact, he wasn't aware of it.

'Well, it would have made all the difference to me in my day,' Margot told her colleagues. 'I could have kept coming to work. *I'd* have been the CEO by now. Instead, I had this dreadful struggle to keep going, and in the end it was easier to just stay at home with the twins and raise them poor. Good on you, Sam.'

Ellie looked around in alarm from where she was adjusting the screen. Sam had just walked in. Margot's rather penetrating voice immediately caught his attention, and to Ellie's horror he strolled over to her. He frowned and bent to look at the page they were all poring over. Ellie heard him say, 'A what? Where does it say that?'

With her heart in her throat, she watched Sam pick up the booklet. He leaned casually on a side table to scan it, then raised his eyes. From across the room his accusing gaze lasered to clash with hers. The enormity of what she'd done resounded in her head, and she felt the guilt rise to her cheeks in flaming neon. But pride wouldn't allow her to lower her eyes to a man who'd called her his dream girl and made frenzied love to her. Though blistered from head to toe, she held his gaze.

A cover story. For God's sake, why couldn't her fertile brain deliver? She was still racking her brains for one when her old ex-boss, Stephen Fletcher, swanned in.

'Hello all,' Fletcher said, dumping his briefcase, somehow not noticing Sam at the other end of the room. Then, beaming and holding out his hands, 'Ellie, my love.' He made a big production of looking her over and whistling. 'Now, don't you look scrumptious?' He swung a portly arm around her and gave her a hug. 'Still running the bank? From the top now, eh?'

'*Fletcher.*'

The deep, brusque voice fractured the air like a whiplash. Fletcher started away from her as if he'd been shot, and conversations dribbled to a close. All heads turned.

Samos Stilakos had taken his power position at the front. In his elegant dark suit, his imposing height, powerful shoulders and strong masculine eyebrows emphasised his authority. 'If you wouldn't mind taking your hands off Ms O'Dea…' He spoke coolly, but his imperious eyes held dagger points. He pointed Fletcher to a vacant chair. 'Sit. Please.'

The *please* was an obvious afterthought.

Poor Fletcher's face crumpled. An embarrassed hush fell on the assembled group.

Sam nodded forbiddingly towards Ellie. 'Eleanor. The doors.'

She strolled to close them as casually as she could, sensing his gaze follow her every move from beneath his bristling brows. When she slipped into her own chair, she couldn't restrain herself from sending him a scathing glance for his treatment of her old boss.

Despite an icy look in return, Sam delivered his presentation in a relaxed style, like the professional he was. It went over well with the managers, who hadn't warmed to him when he'd first taken over the bank and cut so many of their perks. Now they applauded him, appreciating at last that they had a competent and dynamic leader at the helm.

He hardly looked her way, although a few times she had the definite sense he wanted to, but when he did flick her a glance his chiselled mouth was stern, his eyes coolly unreadable. He'd never looked more handsome. More smoulderingly sexy.

She kept her spine stiff, hyper-conscious of the things she'd said to him. Why should she feel so guilty? *He* should be guilty. It wasn't as if he'd said he loved her, was it? So why did she have to feel this huge, unswallowable lump in her chest?

What right did a man have to demand honesty from a woman anyway, just because he'd said a few romantic things?

He directed some occasional comments to her. They were smoothly polite, even considerate, on the surface. Only she could detect the biting under-edge. Once, when she reached for the water, several of the men sprang to assist her but Sam interrupted his talk to smoothly swoop on the carafe first. He poured her a glass and handed it to her with extreme courtesy, taking care not to touch her fingers.

Briefly their eyes clashed, his glinting, perhaps with some memory of a similar moment last night. Unless… Her unquiet blood stirred. Could he have been thinking of the car park? Was the potent scene still as raw in his senses as it was in hers— their greedy kisses, their avid lips and hands?

She fought the image off with a little shiver. It was ironic. The managers seemed more at ease with him than ever before, though that only made it worse. Before they broke up, to her horror someone felt confident enough to revive the discussion about the on-site crèche. Too clever not to recognise its value as an ice-breaker, Sam allowed the topic to continue, sitting seemingly relaxed, his lean, tanned hands lightly resting on the table.

Hands that had caressed her. Hands even now she wanted to reach out and touch.

The pros and cons of small babies in childcare were being robustly canvassed.

Sam listened to the debate with half an ear. His glance fell on *her*, a couple of simmering metres across from him, black lace at her breast, her long hair catching the light. She appeared to be listening attentively, but there was a rigidity in her posture. He grimaced. *Let* her be nervous. As though sensing his scrutiny, she angled her face away from him. The distinctive tilt of her head, the curve of her cheek, grabbed at something in his chest.

His jaw tightened. She was a mystery.

Ellie forced herself not to glance at him, though superimposed on her brain was the recurring image of his stunned face at her front door. So she'd used a convenient lie. What else could she have done? Would he have enjoyed a heart-to-heart about her ovaries?

She made an effort to tune into the discussion. One of the firm's old dinosaurs was opposed to mothers working in any circumstances and had aroused a storm of debate.

'We need a younger woman's point of view,' Margot asserted, looking around. 'What do you think, Ellie? Could you imagine bringing your baby to work with you?'

Ellie's heart froze. All eyes turned on her, including Sam's. She had the sensation of her stomach dropping several storeys. This was the last thing—the *last* thing—she could discuss in his presence. In other circumstances she'd have loved to run this discussion, with these very same people, and knew she could do it well. But not in front of Sam. Not—for God's sake—after last night.

She avoided his eyes, in dread of seeing his lip curl, but still she felt his burning gaze sear her face like an oxy-acetylene torch. Oblivious to the undercurrents, the managers were fired up to persuade her to their points of view. Unknown to them, every word they said wounded her tender sensibility like napalm.

'Ellie won't want to work if she has a baby, will you, Ellie? She'll want to stay home and look after the kid properly, like any decent mother.'

'Rubbish, Gary,' Margot said testily. 'Women have the right to work. Ellie's a career girl through and through. She won't want to give it up for nappies and milky vomit. She'll go for having it all, won't you, Ellie? The job *and* the family.'

'Why can't her husband support her until the child goes to school?'

'He mightn't have a job. *She* might be the breadwinner.'

'It wouldn't work to bring a baby here,' someone growled. 'Too much distraction from the job. She'd be better off to put the kid in a nursery down the street.'

The arguments grew even more excruciating.

'But what if she wants to breast-feed?'

'Then she shouldn't have a baby unless she's in a position to do it.'

The discussion raged. All the way through it she could feel the weight of Sam's scrutiny burning a pathway into her quivering soul. Finally one of them stopped arguing long enough to notice her frozen silence. 'Look at poor Ellie. Here we are grilling her when she hasn't even begun to think of babies yet. Give the girl a break.'

The combined forces of all their eyes turned on her again.

Panic gripped her throat. She knew what they were all thinking. They were assessing her age, speculating about her love-life and her diminishing chances. Her ovaries were in the spotlight. In a moment some wit would mention the biological clock, and tell her to get a move on and find Mr Right.

It was the career girl's worst nightmare.

Normally, when public exposure or boss trouble threatened, she could summon a serene smile and handle it with aplomb. But right then she couldn't. For once she experienced performance failure. Her face felt stiff, and she knew her eyes were glassy.

She managed to push herself up on her high heels, and say with jerky dignity, 'If you'll all excuse me, there are some things I have to do.' With a bright, unfocused smile around at the assembly, she walked swiftly from the room, closed the door behind her and sprinted like an Olympic athlete for the Ladies.

After a few drastic minutes of hyperventilation—in lieu of a paper bag she had to bunch up a paper towel and pant into that—she dashed cold water on her face, and tried to pat it dry without disturbing her make-up. This was the worst day of her life so far, and she'd brought it all on herself. Her small effort to improve entitlements for the bank's workforce had blown up in her face.

She couldn't bear to imagine what Sam was thinking of her after she'd so seriously betrayed his trust. And how mortifying, how utterly humiliating, that he'd witnessed her crumble like that. How much had he guessed about her? Her soul screamed with embarrassment. She felt ready to burrow a hole in the tiles and bury herself there. That a man, a sexual partner, a l—she shied from the L word—should see her in the light of a desperate spinster.

It took some heavy-duty slow, concentrated breathing to bring her pulse-rate back to a point approaching normal, so she could start to think.

She had to face it. She was definitely in the wrong over that booklet. The knowledge was unbearable, but how to right herself in his eyes? Her usual tactic of a sincere explanation with a lorryload of charm hardly seemed adequate this time. How would she justify *this*?

And after last night, the issue was so complicated. Shouldn't she apologise, just this once? Throw herself on his mercy, show him she had a conscience about insulting him and hurting his feelings? Crawl on her hands and knees to beg his forgiveness?

She left the sanctuary of the ladies' room with a half-formed plan of humbly admitting she was at fault, grovelling, and somehow appealing to his sense of fairness to leave the events of last night out of the equation.

As she approached the entrance to her office a burst of laughter reached her from the hall. With a jealous pang, she saw it was the group of managers, congregating in front of the lifts, exchanging what sounded like light-hearted banter with Sam. Judging by the approving glances they were giving him, rapport had been established. They were all basking in the sunshine of his smile. Even Fletcher looked to have been charmed into the fold.

She'd never felt so excluded in her life. She made the painful acknowledgement to herself that she'd do anything to have Sam smile at her like that again.

He caught sight of her and his face smoothed to become expressionless. 'Oh, there you are.' He detached himself from his worshippers and strode purposefully towards her. 'Come in here.' He opened his office door. 'We need to talk.'

She accompanied him tremulously, some weak part of her longing to abase herself, kiss his gorgeous bronzed feet and ankles and beg forgiveness, but another, stronger part knowing it was a mistake to ever acknowledge to a boss that he had the upper hand.

He halted in the middle of the room and confronted her, his lean, handsome face stern, his sensuous mouth compressed. He was quite close to her, as the crow flew, but somehow the small distance between them was sharply defined, like an unbridgeable chasm. Unfortunately, her body didn't understand what her mind knew, and surged with shameless longing for him to touch her.

'We need to get some things straight,' he said. 'Are you on the pill?'

She blenched. 'What?'

His sardonic brows lifted. 'Oh, it's the innocent maiden routine.'

She flinched as from a physical blow.

His dark eyes flickered over her in merciless condemnation as he said softly, 'Let me remind you, Eleanor, that you had unprotected sex last night. In a car park. I find it hard to believe that any woman, even a woman prone to screwing in such casual venues, wouldn't be alive to the risks.'

Her sensibilities felt savaged, but feminine honour demanded she defend herself. 'The possibilities of infection, do you mean?' she countered coldly. 'Yes, I am aware of it, and I intend to have a medical check at the first opportunity.'

A muscle tightened in his jaw and she knew she'd scored.

'I can take it, then, you are using a contraceptive?' His eyes were unfriendly. 'Considering that little discussion you took it upon yourself to engineer, it seemed reasonable to assume when you exited like that…a panicked gazelle springs to mind…that you might be fearful of being pregnant.'

She gave him a cold smile. 'I'm not fearful. There's no need to concern yourself.'

It was true. Pregnancy was probably the only thing left in life she wasn't concerned about. It was only two months since she'd given up using the pill, and with her ovaries, the chances of her conceiving so soon, if ever, were infinitesimal. Possibly non-existent.

'I can assure you,' she added sweetly, '*you* have nothing to worry about.'

She could tell by Sam's wintry expression the insinuation hadn't been lost on him. Anger flared in his eyes, and for a moment she thought he might seize her.

Goaded, Sam felt his hands twitch. He read the flash of uncertainty in her blue eyes, and clenched them to his sides. Touching her was now forbidden. With frustration he surveyed her slender form in the slim dress, her long legs fragilely balanced on the precarious shoes.

Her skin had never looked so meltingly soft and delicate as it did against the black lace trim. That white swell of breast just visible at the bodice was fatally desirable, or *would* have been if… He felt rising wrath. Where did a woman learn to be so unpredictable, so stubbornly intent on twisting things her way, so *difficult*?

Dammit, he was a man and he was in charge.

'My only concern is for your health and well-being,' he snapped. 'I wanted to assure you that, should a messy situation occur, you would be taken care of.'

Ellie wondered who would do the care-taking. Would he go with her himself, or send his chauffeur, or his housekeeper? 'I can imagine,' she said with heavy irony.

His eyes flashed, and he said very quietly, '*I* can only imagine what sort of men you've been with in the past, Eleanor, that you have such a low regard for them.'

She wanted to cover her face to protect herself from the shaming insults raining down on her. Instead she turned away from him. 'Is that all you wanted to say?'

'That's only the beginning.' He strolled right around her to plant his big, powerful frame in front of her and force her to look at him. 'I'd like to remind you that you aren't in control of this bank. What's more, this is a *bank*, not a testing ground for women's social agendas. Whatever your bosses tolerated from you in the past, for the pleasure of looking at you every day, won't be tolerated in this office. *I* am in control here.'

She gasped at the insult, but this was so much more the kind of fight she could handle. Her adrenaline surged and, along with it, her courage. Courage to justify, justify, justify!

'Of course I know you're in charge,' she said in a shocked, wounded tone, and added with quick sincerity, 'I can explain what happened, Sam. I knew how keen you were to find an issue that would bring the managers on-side. The crèche idea seemed ideal, being so controversial to their old-fashioned ways of thinking, without personally threatening any of them, and just the sort of thing you would choose yourself. I had intended to run it by you yesterday, but with all that happened—' Her voice grew huskier as an involuntary flashback to the car park nearly melted her defiance. 'It—it—I'm afraid it completely slipped my mind.'

She flashed a glance at him, but there was no softening in the severe lines of his chiselled, sexy mouth. She dropped her lashes and made a conciliatory gesture. 'Perhaps you're right. The idea might be just a bit too—*out* there for this bank.'

It was a subtle shot, and she could tell it registered by the way his eyes glinted. She followed it up with an appealing gaze through her lashes. 'You did say you liked PAs to show initiative. I suppose I must have misunderstood what that meant.'

His eyes chilled to ice. 'That is not the issue here.' He whisked the ball from her hands by stating with relentless accuracy, 'This is about a breach of trust, isn't it, Eleanor?'

The blood rushed to her face as if she'd been slapped.

'And there is the little matter of dress. Since when have you felt the need to come to work dressed like a tart?'

She gasped, but he went on inexorably. 'I may not know everything about fashion, but it's obvious to me that dress isn't appropriate for the workplace. It looks like something you should be wearing with a suspender belt and lace-topped stockings. Why aren't you wearing a suit?'

She said stiffly, 'My suit is in the Porsche.'

He paused. 'Oh. The Porsche.' For a moment the space between them simmered. She had visions of his hot hands on her thighs, her rapid panting breath, their urgent coupling in the pungent, salty air.

His eyes darkened and he turned abruptly away from her. 'It would be a mistake to try to capitalise on anything that happened between us out of working hours. I don't want a secretary who advertises her charms. I expect my PA to be a role-model of modesty and elegance to the remainder of the workforce.'

She bristled with indignation. Her beautiful dress *was* modest and elegant. She thought of the hole in her hard-won savings, what that meant now to her precious timeline, all the little deprivations ahead, the waiting, the sheer sacrifice, and rebellion boiled up in her. 'This,' she snapped, 'is an extremely expensive dress by a world-famous Australian designer. It's a work of art. It even has its own title.'

He turned to sweep her with a gaze of satiric amusement. 'Really. And what title would that be?'

Her blood pressure jumped a couple of notches, but she said coolly enough, 'It's called Flirty Noir.'

'Forgive me. A *French* tart.'

The insufferable mockery stung, but still she hung onto her temper. 'Other people like it.'

His eyes flared dangerously. '*Other* people. You mean Fletcher. And the rest of your fan club who couldn't keep their eyes off you. Ogling you at every chance they got. I'm sure they did like it. They don't have to work in close proximity to you.'

She felt a hot rush to her head that set her very scalp on fire. 'And that's what *you* want, isn't it?' she taunted in breathless anger. 'More proximity.'

He grabbed her and pushed her up against his desk. She felt a furious, excited thrill as he brought his mouth down on hers, and clung to him, relishing the ferocious hunger of his searing lips as her bones liquefied and passion instantly ignited her blood. She kissed him back, as fierce and fervent as he, her hands flying to undo his shirt buttons, his belt buckle, wriggling in frantic urgency to assist him to drag down her zip, unfasten her bra.

She positioned herself on the edge of the desk, her knees parted for him, the breath coming in quick little pants as he pulled the dress from her shoulders and laid her straining breasts bare. For an intense, electric instant he stared down at her, lust in the black eyes feasting on her white nakedness. Drenched in desire, she quivered on the verge of the wild ride to rapture, her nipples taut and aching, fever between her thighs.

Through his open shirt, his broad bronzed chest with its smattering of black hairs tantalised her unbearably. In her impatience, she leaned forward and gave his nipple a long, languorous lick.

A shock roiled through his body. His hands tightened fiercely on her shoulders, then, with an almost superhuman effort, he thrust her from him and swerved away. She lost her balance and half fell backwards. He stood with his back to her, his hands bunched into fists, sinews straining in his powerful neck and shoulders.

'Dress yourself.' The words were as raw as if they'd been wrenched from him. Their disdain cut her to the quick.

A tidal wave of shame suffused her. She slid off the desk and reassembled her clothes with clumsy, trembling hands. How could her body have so betrayed her? How could she have shown herself so ready to surrender?

Sam fought for the strength to shut her from his consciousness, and waited for desire to subside. He struggled not to smell her fragrance, not to think of smooth breasts aching for a man's hands, of firm, slim thighs edged by black lace.

His father's stern, honest face flashed before him and he winced. Self-disgust rose in his throat like bile. He was no better than the series of greedy, lecherous executives who'd brought the bank close to ruin.

How had he, Samos Stilakos, come to this? When had a woman ever brought him so low?

He heard the door close, and felt overwhelmed by a guilty sensation of relief.

Shaky, disoriented, Ellie stood outside, her face in her hands, mind and body a painful, aching turmoil. She sat down at her desk and stared blindly at her keyboard. Despair would settle in soon enough, she thought. What man had ever treated her with such contempt?

She stayed outside until her hands stopped shaking, and the blood ceased pounding her temples, then forced herself to go in to face him.

He was helping himself to a drink from the water cooler, his clothes once more immaculate, every movement as controlled as if nothing had happened. He strolled to his desk, paper cup in hand, and flicked her a look. Just for an instant, she thought she caught uncertainty in his glittering black glance.

She lifted her chin, not wanting him to see how vulnerable she felt.

'This can't go on,' he rasped. 'It has to stop. I can't have this.'

'You don't have to worry.' Her own voice was equally emotionally charged. 'Because as of this moment, I quit.'

A muscle twitched in his lean cheek and he stood still, looking at her for a second with a fathomless gaze, then he coolly sat down. 'That might be the best solution all round.'

He picked up a pencil and twirled it idly between his lean fingers. It snapped. He straightened his cuffs, and, without looking at her again, pulled out his computer keyboard. 'You might as well clear out your desk.'

He became immersed in his screen.

Outside, she covered her face with her hands and succumbed to a major shaking fit. Her legs gave way and she plumped down on her chair. She opened and shut her desk drawers a few times, then reached for an empty copy-paper carton. She stacked some useless things into it, tipped them out and started again.

After a few minutes the door opened and Sam came out. He took a few strides past her desk, then stopped as if he'd remembered something. 'Your contract requires you to give a month's notice,' he said in a cold voice.

She kept her gaze lowered. 'I'm leaving now.'

'If you do that you'll lose your severance entitlements.'

'Think of the profit to your bank,' she suggested.

He was silent for a moment, then said in a dry, steady voice, 'You will still have to come back to pick up your reference.'

She kept her head down. 'I won't be needing one from you, thanks. I have wonderful references from my previous bosses.'

His feet paused in front of her desk, then he strode back inside and shut the door with a snap.

When she'd piled as much as she could carry into the carton, she stood up with it in her arms and hoisted her bag onto her shoulder. The door burst open and Sam came out.

'Eleanor.' He stood directly in front of her so she was forced to meet his eyes.

Coldly, proudly, she faced her adversary.

'If you—if you did find yourself in a difficult situation—a crisis, like a—an unplanned pregnancy, for example, what would you do?'

Despite her anger with him his eyes were serious, as if he was genuinely concerned, and confusion welled in her heart. Why did he have to remind her of how he'd been before he hated her? A multitude of the glib, savage things she could have said sprang to her tongue and died there. Whatever she was, she was a woman, and she had a heart.

With icy dignity she said, 'I would see it as a situation requiring a practical solution, and I would deal with it.'

The lines of his face tautened. 'How?' He added drily, 'Or can I guess?' With a grimace he half turned away. 'No, don't tell me.'

Her anger sparked back to life and she flung him a withering glance. 'Is it so obvious?' She slung her bag onto her shoulder and started for the exit. 'I'd find a job in a company that cares about its workforce and has an on-site crèche.'

He strode after her, grabbed her arm and pulled her about to face him. 'Understand this, darling,' he bit out through clenched teeth. 'No child of mine will ever be dragged up in a public facility.'

Darling. That caught her on the raw.

She arched her brows and flashed him a cruel smile. 'No child you know about, perhaps.'

CHAPTER EIGHT

ELLIE'S state of shock lasted until she got home. Once the front door was closed behind her she peeled off her dress, collapsed on her bed and gave way to the huge black hole that had opened in her chest.

Afterwards, trying not to visualise Sam's cold eyes, she hauled herself up, changed into jeans, washed her blotchy face and tied her hair behind with a ribbon. She threw herself into some therapeutic house-cleaning, until she felt in enough control of her emotions to phone Beth to tell her the catastrophic news. Shocked, Beth promised to come over after work for a full report.

She drifted to the computer and half-heartedly keyed into a job-search site, but it was too painful. It only reminded her of how much she loved working at the bank. Surely she was a permanent fixture there. Wasn't she famous throughout the departments? So many of her friends were there.

He was there.

She still couldn't believe she'd thrown it all away. She stared miserably at the pile of things in the hall, then knelt to repack them in preparation for sending back to the shop.

How had she come to make such a mess of things? She tried to think it all through with clear-headed logic, but Sam's furious face swam constantly before her eyes.

She couldn't imagine not seeing him every day. From the day

he'd summoned her to the interview she'd been riding on a high. She closed her eyes and let herself dwell on her loss. The emotional impact of their first meeting each morning. Those charged moments at staff meetings when their gazes met. His deep, smooth tones on the intercom.

How flat her life would be now without it all.

If only she hadn't been forced to reject him last night.

But surely, all wasn't lost. Of course this morning she'd lost her temper, they'd both been carried away, but couldn't the situation be retrieved? It was obvious the passion between them was a living thing. Surely that must work to her advantage. And with her experience of talking bosses round, how hard could it be to persuade him she was worth another chance? If she went to see him in the morning and admitted her fault, apologised as she should have done today, instead of scoring points…

If only, if only she could have another chance…

She had a daydream that he would leave work and come in search of her. He'd beg her to come back, he'd apologise for the cruel things he'd said. Instead of being cool, clever Ms O'Dea she'd show him how she truly felt underneath. When he took her in his arms and kissed her she would…

Later, Beth brought over some chocolate éclairs to commiserate, and they sat in her little courtyard garden at the back while Ellie poured out the events of the last twenty-four hours.

True to form, Beth put her finger straight on the point at which things had gone bad. 'Couldn't you have just whisked all that IVF information out of sight?' Her green eyes were wide with incredulity. 'Stuffed it in a drawer or something?'

'It was too much of a risk. He might have seen it. He's very astute. He doesn't miss a thing. You don't know what he's like. He's—' Her throat thickened and she couldn't trust herself to go on.

Beth wanted to see the two dresses. 'They're both gorgeous, but this, *this*. Oh-h,' she moaned softly, fingering the black one. 'To *die* for. But it's far too good for work.' She examined

Ellie with a rueful gaze. 'You didn't buy this just for the sake of your job, did you?'

Ellie shook her head without speaking, afraid of bursting into tears.

Beth stayed until after dark, then helped her clear up the coffee things, and left with sympathetic instructions to phone if she needed to talk more. After waving her off, Ellie was still standing at the front window, staring at the empty street, when a car nosed into the kerb in front of her gate.

It was sleek, dark and expensive-looking. Her heart gave a hopeful, joyous bound. She dashed to the bathroom to tidy her hair and met her anxious eyes in the mirror, huge and shadowy in her white face, their colour intensified by the deep blue of her tee shirt. When the bell rang her knees suddenly felt watery, and she had to discipline herself to walk to the door calmly.

Sam stood there with a carrier bag dangling from one hand. He was still in his office clothes and his lean face was serious and controlled, his severely sculpted mouth firm, black eyebrows slightly drawn. He looked the epitome of a powerful businessman. He flicked a veiled glance over her, taking in her jeans and shirt, then fastened his sharp gaze to her face. He made the slightest movement towards her. For a wild, fluttering moment she thought he was going to kiss her, but instead he just handed her the bag.

'Your things.'

'Thanks.' Her voice came out strangely, as if she'd been in a cave for twenty years without speaking. 'I— Would you—?' She cleared her throat. 'Please. Come in.'

She opened the door wide. His eyes glinted, and she knew he was thinking of last night. After a second's hesitation, he followed her down the hall and into her sitting room. For a tense, silent moment he stood facing her. His eyes were dark and sexual, and she felt an overwhelming desire to lace her arms around his neck and press herself into his big, hard body, but pride forced her to control it.

He sat down on her red sofa without touching her, his feet planted authoritatively apart in their hand-stitched Italian shoes, his intelligent eyes alert. She sank onto a chair facing him.

He glanced around at her bookshelves and pictures, the occasional photos she kept of family and friends, then switched his gaze back to her. His eyes travelled down her throat to the neck of her top, and she was overwhelmingly conscious of her bed, just visible through the half-open door to her bedroom, a few short metres away across the hall.

He wouldn't have come if he didn't want her. The knowledge drummed in her blood and swelled her breasts, and she had to force her hands still, to stop from reaching out to touch him. This was the moment to make her pitch, or lose everything.

'I'm so glad you came, Sam,' she said huskily. 'There are things I need to say.'

'There are things *I* need to say.'

'First I want to apologise—'

He raised imperious eyebrows, and she was silenced.

'No. I want to apologise.' He frowned down at his linked hands and drew a deep breath. 'I want to acknowledge that you were right in those things you said last night. I strongly regret the entire evening. What happened, and the way—the *place* it happened.' His hands lifted, eloquent of distaste. 'I blame myself. And—today. I should not have—exploited my working relationship with you in that way. You were my PA, and I should not have given in to… It was all my fault.' He looked up at her then lowered his black lashes and said quietly, 'You made the right decision.'

A shock wave roiled through her. She felt her life's blood drain from her heart.

'By—by quitting, do you mean? You're saying—it's a good thing I did?'

His eyes held hers with daunting firmness of purpose. 'I've written you a reference.' He nodded towards the carrier bag. 'It's in there with your things. In view of your long service with the bank, you will certainly receive all your severance and holiday pays.'

She was so stunned she could barely speak, but she couldn't just leave it at that. She gave a small, disbelieving laugh and made a weak gesture of appeal. 'I—I had thought—wondered, if you might try to talk me into changing my mind.'

'I'd like to.' His eyes on her face were grave. 'You're an excellent PA and I'll miss your input. You have skills and ability far in advance of PA work. In fact, I believe you can do better.' He dropped his gaze, and added quietly in his dark chocolate voice, 'And after what's developed between us on a personal level, Eleanor, I think you'll agree we can't work together any more.'

Her heart lurched. There was a buzzing in her head, as if all her worst-case scenarios had ganged up to confront her at the same time. 'So you—you don't want me back at the bank tomorrow?'

He looked gravely at her. 'Understand, I'd love to have you back. But it's not good for the bank when the CEO looks forward to seeing one face every day.' His voice softened. 'There is another of the Stilakos companies on the lookout for an executive PA, with opportunities for advancement to management. The salary is very attractive, better than what you were earning…'

Shock had sandbagged her brain to dullness, but her pride still had a vestige of life. She said with a stiff gesture, 'I can find my own position, thank you.'

He was silent for a moment, his dark eyes veiled. He examined her face, then lowered his gaze. 'Of course, of course. I know you can. You'll do well. With your talents and experience…'

Her mouth twisted. 'My pretty face…'

A flush tinged the olive skin covering his cheekbones. 'I—' He checked and made a stilted gesture. 'I shouldn't have said that. That was unfair. You're much, much more than…' With a stern effort he straightened his posture and met her eyes firmly. 'I take full responsibility for everything that has happened.'

Pain and disappointment closed around her heart like a vice, and she looked down at her hands. 'Tell me. Is this—is this really because of the crèche thing?'

'No.' His voice thickened. 'It's because of the passion thing.'

She turned her eyes away to hide them from him. Irrational, weak as it may have seemed, she longed for him to take her in his arms and comfort her for the hurt and desolation he was causing her. 'So, I'm just another statistic, after all,' she managed to say lightly, though the stranglehold on her heart made her voice hoarse.

Despite the cruelty of it, some treacherous part of her brain acknowledged the truth of what he was saying. There was no turning back the clock to the time when they hadn't made love. Everything between them now, every word, every gesture, was imbued with her almost tangible memory of his strong arms, his mouth and hands on her skin. Even now, while he was chopping her insides into little pieces, she craved for him to touch her.

But true to her feminine spirit, on the outside, at least, she kept her spine taut and her chin up, and stood up to signal him it was time to leave.

He rose with reluctance, as if racking his brains for what else he might say to help her swallow the bitter hemlock.

She gathered all the pride at her disposal and faced him coldly. 'You should know the passion thing was only ever a temporary aberration. It no longer exists. Thank you for calling.'

He shook his head and made a move to touch her, but she raised her hands to ward him off. 'Don't,' she said fiercely.

His eyes blazed. 'I'm sure, when you've had time to think, Eleanor, you'll realise this is the best way. How long do you think it would be before other people began to realise we couldn't keep our hands off each other?' He gesticulated passionately. 'Today I came close to having you on my desk. How long before we're taking afternoons off, missing meetings, locking my door to keep other people out while we make love? Everything is noticed and discussed at the bank; you said so yourself. This is not what I want for *us*.' His brilliant black eyes glittered and his deep voice took on a sharp, stern edge. Light glanced from his proud cheekbones, his firm jaw. His Greek heritage had never been more clearly defined. 'I am not a man who conducts affairs in his office. And you are not the kind of woman to enjoy being gossiped about.' He looked like the severe, uncompromising Samos Stilakos who'd commanded the workforce's respect. *Her* respect.

'You're assuming an awful lot,' she said in a low, trembling voice. 'You're assuming I'd be a willing participant.'

Sensuality stirred the depths of the dark eyes fixed on her face. 'I am, yes,' he said softly. 'I am assuming that.'

The naked desire in his gaze pierced her and she weakened. Longing for him rose in her to war with her embattled pride. He was only a metre's distance from her. She could reach out to him, press her mouth to the strong bronzed column of his neck. He would seize her and the dark flame would flare and consume both of them. She felt the dangerous erotic surge, and knew if he touched her she would surrender to the blaze, even as he was destroying her.

But how easily a man discarded a woman, even one he desired. And what foolish arrogance had ever deluded her into dreaming she could have the upper hand with Samos Stilakos? The bitter realisations clamoured in her brain. Her breasts rose and fell with the intensity of her struggle, and with her voice hoarse and trembling, she said, 'Whatever it was that happened between us is over, Sam. Thank you for returning my things.'

His lean dark face was focused and intense, his eyes ardent. 'It's not over. We have hardly begun. You're upset now, under-standably, but when you cool down you'll see. We both know the passion between us. If I touch you…even now, if I touch you, if we…' He took her arms in his firm, warm hands. 'We're meant to be lovers. I want you with me every night.'

She cried, 'You must be joking.' She gave a violent twist and tore herself from his grasp. Angry tears sprang to her eyes. 'The bank has been like my second home all the years I've worked there. Do you think this is nothing to me, losing my job? My *life*? And can you seriously believe I would want to carry on as your—toy? Can you imagine that after today I would ever want to see you again?' She brushed back her hair with impatient, shaking hands. 'You can have no idea—*no idea!*—of how much I have put into my work there. Of how much—over—over the years—I have *done*—' Emotion took control of her voice and she was forced to stop to take a series of breaths.

She caught a fleeting, almost unrecognisable glimpse of herself in the hall mirror, her face dead white, her eyes glittering with blue fire, and turned from the unbearable sight.

Sam said, harsh bitterness in his deep voice, 'Oh, I assure you, I am well aware of the sacrifices some women are prepared to make for their careers.'

'Just—just look at what has happened here,' she carried on in her distress as if he hadn't spoken. 'How are you different from all those big-time executives who ran the bank into the ground? And *I*—I know I've been just as stupid as all those sec-retaries. How could I? How could I have allowed myself to—?' She dashed away a tear with the back of her hand. More tears choked her throat.

The lines of his lean strong face clenched. Fire blazed in his eyes. He breathed harshly. 'What has happened between us has nothing to do with other people. It is unique to you and me. If you can't see that I am different from those men…I don't have woman after woman. I only want…'

He drew a long simmering breath. After a moment he said, his deep voice uneven despite his effort of control, 'We need to talk about this rationally. You need to grow used to the idea of changing your employment, then we can talk about the kind of relationship we want. It doesn't have to be difficult for you to find a new place. I want to help you.'

Such cynical promises, while all she'd striven to achieve lay in smoking ruins, swept away the last vestiges of her self-pos-session.

'Oh, please.' She wiped her brow with a trembling hand. 'You don't have to pretend this is anything but what it is. A sordid office affair you want out of. Don't worry. I want nothing more to do with you in my life.'

His handsome face tautened. He gave a cool shrug, then swung stiffly for the door.

At the front door he paused with his hand on the knob, his shoulders rigidly set, then turned to scan her face. 'You'll find another position without trouble, I promise.'

'I'm sure I can rely on that.'

He lowered his thick black lashes, but not before she saw his eyes flash. He said through gritted teeth, 'Believe it or not, I *do* honour promises if I can.'

Her glance fell on the boxes of vain, frivolous clothes still awaiting the courier, and she nudged them with the toe of her shoe. 'I hope you know I'm sending these things back to the shop.'

'Why? Keep them. I want you to have them.'

Her voice trembled. 'I'd rather not feel like some rich man's mistress.'

He tensed and paused on her doorstep, his eyes chill and stern, and said quietly, 'I hope any woman fortunate enough to be my mistress, Eleanor, would also be gracious enough to know how to accept a gift in the spirit in which it is given.'

He spun on his heel and walked away.

Out of her life.

CHAPTER NINE

TILL hell freezes over, Sam thought.

Still, he kept his cool. He opened his car door, slid into his seat, snapped on the seat belt, every movement measured. He inserted the key and fired the ignition, not a tremor in his fingers. With controlled precision he drove to the end of the street, slowed at the lights.

A tidal wave of black emotion rose up to engulf him. His hands clenched the wheel.

Women didn't reject him. Not twice. He winced. Not *once*. The lights turned green and he slammed his foot to the floor.

He would have her. He would have his fill of her and she would be grateful. She'd crawl to him for more. She'd be on her knees, sobbing for an affair with him.

He sped through a small local shopping precinct and screamed the car to a halt at a street-crossing. A lone female pedestrian, paralysed in the middle of the crossing, turned an outraged glare into his headlights.

He yanked at his tie and loosened his shirt collar. He had done the only possible thing. So why did he feel like such a bastard?

Of course she was upset. It was only natural. She'd lost her job. If he was guilty of anything it was of having underestimated just how upset she would be. He thought back to the moment when she'd first opened the door to him, the joyous expectation in her sapphire eyes, and his heart twisted.

For a moment he longed to do anything, *anything* to wipe away the pain he'd caused her. Drive back there, give her the job, set it all straight, turn back the clock…

Bleak dismay swept through him at the vision of her once-tranquil face, twisted in outrage and despair.

How would he ever retrieve himself in her eyes?

CHAPTER TEN

IT WAS shattering to find how soon she could be forgotten by friends, people she'd worked with for years.

In the days following the crisis they phoned, dying to know what was behind her departure. Ellie sensed the avidness in some of the enquiries. People fishing for gossip, hoping to hear some juicy scandal about her and Sam. It was humiliating, but she put on a bright performance, and pretended to have decided on a change in career.

All too soon, though, the calls began to drop off.

With frightening speed her bank world started to recede, and she guessed the reverse would also be true. Even the most popular staff member could leave, with barely a ripple to disturb the daily functioning of the big machine.

Sam didn't recede. Not in her mind, at least. Night after night she agonised over her last scene with him, raw with pain that he'd put his personal honour and reputation ahead of her happiness and security.

She didn't care who was right. Or that she was the one who'd resigned, she was the one who'd insisted on bringing in ethics, and she had been an equal and willing sexual partner. What she needed was for him to suffer as she was suffering. And to care, and feel sorry. And to crawl on his knees to beg her forgiveness, while she ground him into the earth with her heel.

But he didn't contact her. He didn't call to see how she was, or to check if she had anything to tell him about work, or to enquire about meetings and appointments.

It was cruelly frustrating, because she wanted to punish him properly. Shout and scream at him, shake him and show him how it felt to be cut to ribbons. And she wanted him to give her her job back, and make the terrifying pain better, as though it had never happened.

As two weeks turned to three his implacable silence slammed home the finality of his goodbye, and her anger turned to herself. How could she have allowed herself to fall into the same old trap? Once again she'd been beguiled by a man's charm, only this time the consequences had wiped her out. She'd wasted her savings, and it had been her own fault. She'd had a goal, she'd made sacrifices for it, and she'd allowed herself to be tempted from it.

She'd never fallen in so deep. Her passion for him was like a madness.

She knew she had to fight it, but she was weak. At every turn the shock of her loss asserted itself. Like an addict deprived of the fatal poppy, the touch and feel and taste of him were on her hands and skin as if he were a part of her very fibre.

She tried to fight the constant longing, but couldn't stop willing the phone to ring, running to the window to check every car that drew up in the street. She checked her message bank a dozen times a day; even, in some shamefully low moments, considered texting him, begging him to forgive the terrible things she'd said to him.

But of course he wouldn't. A man like Samos Stilakos would never forgive such a blow to his pride, and she steeled herself to the daunting necessity of rebuilding her life and starting afresh.

Her practical side fastened to the task of getting back on course.

With a mental gritting of teeth, she set her sights on her next job and travelled daily to the city on the round of job interviews. Too proud at first to use it, her reference from Sam, when she eventually relented, opened doors to her that would certainly have been otherwise closed, despite her qualifications.

Weeks after her last conversation with him, she was plunged into a dilemma when a friend from the bank phoned to invite her to a farewell lunch in her honour. Ironically, it had been given the nod of approval from the top.

What did it mean? Her first instinct was to avoid the torture, but her friends didn't deserve such cold treatment. Besides, she would already be in town that day for her second interview with a firm of management consultants. Going back to the place she'd loved would be hard, but how much harder would be the possibility of seeing Sam?

She couldn't quell the pathetic hope that he'd arranged it so he could see her. That should have warned her. Her struggle to put him out of her mind and heart was still too new to be safe. Although, she argued with herself, he might not be there. Why would he be, when she'd told him she never wanted to see him again in her life?

Though if he didn't, if he took her at her word and she missed seeing him, what new vistas of pain would open before her then?

The day was overcast. A storm gathered on the horizon, giving the sultry sky a bruised, brooding quality. After a rocky start, in which anxiety made her feel almost nauseous, she dressed as neatly as she could in her best suit and steeled herself for another Oscar-winning performance.

It must have gone over well with the consultants, for she was scarcely out of the building and into the street before they phoned her to tell her she had the job. That was cheering, at least. Of her friends at the bank only Beth knew the truth behind her departure, and at least now she could honestly tell people she had another job.

Still, as she braced herself to pass through the familiar glass doors into the bank's marble lobby, and smelled the familiar smells of floor polish and copy paper, regret for the world she'd loved welled in her heart.

Her hand hovered over the lift button for Sam's floor. But the certainty of seeing some new lovely queening it at her desk, melting to Sam's velvet tones on her intercom, was too cruel to contemplate. She bypassed it and rode straight to the top.

Determinedly working at his desk, Sam tried not to glance at his screen-clock. Neverthless, in the corner of his eye the hour flashed, then another minute, and another.

What if she didn't come?

The black void that occupied his chest swelled and threatened to engulf the world. It was everywhere—his apartment. This desolate bank...

She'd been true to her word not to contact him. There'd been nothing for weeks. Just a phone call from the boutique to inform him of the return of his gifts. The finality of the rebuff had cut him to the quick. It had been another sign of his clumsiness with her. Everything he'd done, it seemed, had offended her sensibilities. Everything he'd said.

He needed to find the right words. What were the words?

He thought of Natalie, the women he'd known before his marriage, and their greedy passion for expensive fripperies. Things he thought he knew about women had been turned upside down.

The desk phone rang. His insides clenched, but he forced himself to reach for it coolly. 'Yes?'

The party in the restaurant was quite lavish for the new regime. They'd arranged a cake, and achieved a festive air with flowers and gifts. The first thing that struck Ellie's notice was Sam's absence. Her disappointment was cruel, but she concealed it before her friends, who welcomed her with hugs and cheerful enquiries about her new job.

Amazingly though, a few minutes of listening to their small exchanges about current events in the bank already made her feel like an outsider. They toasted her and made speeches, and she forced herself to pretend with all her heart that a career change was what she'd wanted most in the world.

Towards the end a slight hush fell, and people sat straighter in their chairs. Her insides lurched, and she looked up to see the tall, autocratic figure of Sam at the entrance. Her heart swelled with its bitter-sweet knowledge.

His dark eyes skimmed the assembly until they lighted on her. From across the room she saw his lean, strong face tense, then smooth to become expressionless.

He strolled over and greeted her with quiet courtesy.

She tried to respond normally, but her burning awareness of him dominated her every small action. Her heart thudded with stress and she could hardly meet his eyes, she was so conscious of the insulting things she'd said to him at their last meeting. But as always before his workforce, he remained cool and composed. The last time she'd seen him he'd been all steel and fire. Now he was back to steel and velvet. In his elegant suit and crisp white shirt, he'd never looked more handsome, more remote and inaccessible, more achingly desirable.

He'd written a speech, and stood to deliver it in an easy, friendly style, as if he'd often done this sort of thing, and knew exactly the right tone to take.

She listened to all the flattering things he said about her with downcast eyes and a smile to cover her wounds. He must have gone to great trouble to prepare the speech, because he'd unearthed amusing anecdotes about her from years past at the bank that her friends recognised and laughed at uproariously.

Despite her turbulent heart she laughed too. At the end she stood to receive the customary bank gift. As usual it was a watch, and this one had the quiet elegance that signalled expense. Someone had chosen it with care.

Sam held out his hand and she gave him hers. For a brief instant their palms met. At the familiar leap of her untrustworthy pulse she couldn't prevent the quick rush of emotion, and had to lower her gaze to hide the shimmer of tears. He bent to brush her cheek with his lips. The faint masculine roughness of his jaw grazed her skin in a potent reminder of pleasures lost.

She made a pretence of linking the watch around her wrist. Sam saw her difficulty with the clasp and helped her. Her skin surged to his quick, deft fingers and she had to discipline herself to meet his eyes. After the small applause had died down, she didn't trust herself to give a speech of her own, beyond thanking everyone for their thoughtfulness.

Mindful of not overstaying their permitted hour in the boss's presence, people began to make moves back to their work. When the last noisy group had gone, the restaurant staff swarmed in to clear the tables.

She gathered up her gifts and flowers. Unlike everyone else, Sam hadn't yet made the move to leave. She eyed him uncertainly, and he tilted his head to indicate an alcove by the window, out of the way of the waiters. After a second's hesitation she joined him.

The moment grew tense, and they both spoke at the same time. 'Have you—?'

'Do you—?'

They each gave a strained laugh, then Sam started again. 'There's something I need to ask you. Have you remembered your promise to accompany my mother to the wedding?'

'Oh! The wedding.' She had forgotten. With the events of the past weeks it had been pushed to the back of her mind. 'Are you sure you still want me to go? Wouldn't you rather find someone else?' She made a tremulous effort at a smile but her voice caught. 'Sever all undesirable connections?'

Something flickered in his dark eyes. 'There isn't anyone else. My mother is counting on you. She's—fixed now on having you with her.'

'I see. Oh, well, of course, then.' She shrugged in acquiescence. 'I did—I did promise.' She felt her insides knot then as she remembered the cutting things she'd said to him on her doorstep about his promises, and she flushed and turned from his perceptive gaze.

'Look, Sam. I'm sorry I said those things to you the last time we—talked. I was upset at the time… About my job, you understand. But I shouldn't have been so rude.'

'You have nothing to apologise for.'

There was a short, constrained silence. She became conscious of the muted sounds of rattling crockery and bustle from the restaurant kitchen.

He touched her cheek lightly with his knuckle. 'You will settle into your new firm and be happy, Eleanor. I'm sorry it had to be this way.' His voice deepened. 'I'm sorry you've been hurt. That I've—hurt you.'

She felt her throat thicken and said huskily, 'Nice watch. Who chose it?'

'Oh, er—' he made a vague gesture '—a—a man—a jeweller brought some trays up for me—'

'Could those be actual sapphires?'

His hands shot out and he took her arms in his strong grasp. 'This wasn't what you think it was. You know one of us had to leave.' His sardonic brows were drawn, his eyes fierce with concern.

Emotion swelled in her heart. Everything in her yearned to step into his arms and sink into his hard body, let him comfort her and kiss her. But she daredn't risk it.

'I do know.' With a sharp twist she disengaged herself. 'I even know why it had to be me. Don't concern yourself with it. I'm fine, my life is fine, I have a new job and I'll like it just as much as I did the last one.' She forced a smile. 'I couldn't feel more—positive about the future.'

She hoped he hadn't guessed what a lie that was. Her croaky old voice might have told him that all she had in her was pain. She could feel his frowning gaze scouring her face.

'Is that true? Have you really come to terms with everything?'

What did he want from her? Blood? Did he really want to know the anguish she'd suffered when he'd discarded her, the agonies of fear and hope the possibility of seeing him today had put her through?

She knew with sudden certainty she didn't want him to feel guilty. She was to blame as much as he. It was time to walk away with her head high, no hard feelings. It took a supreme effort, even after all her experience. As usual, her voice was the hardest to control.

'I don't deny it's been hard.' Bright, sincere smile, airy shrug, if a bit jerky. 'A change always is. But in the long run it'll do me good. One thing I realised coming here today was that I've been in the one place too long. You were right about that. I needed to climb to higher ground.' Her emotions threatened but she crushed them down. 'It was a—a shame it had to happen that way. But I'm a big girl, I know the score…I always did, and I have no regrets.'

The words seemed somehow to clang in the hushed atmosphere of the restaurant. 'You know the score,' he murmured in echo, with a frown. He glanced at his watch. 'Look, let's go somewhere where we can talk.'

He flicked open his mobile and made a couple of quick calls, then took her arm and ushered her out to the lift. On the drive to his apartment the silence was charged. She glanced at him a couple of times, but his expression was grim, his mouth unsmiling.

The apartment was bathed in a dim hush, in waiting for its master. Sam opened some blinds and windows to let in the sultry afternoon, then turned to her. 'Drink?'

She shook her head, but he poured one for himself, half raised it, then put it down again, and loosened his tie.

'Come this way. Please. Through here.'

She followed him uncertainly through the archway, into a suite of rooms. He showed her to a sitting room, which opened into a light, spacious bedroom with furnishings that were essentially masculine, including an opulent bed. A glass ceiling dome above it gave a thrilling glimpse of stormy sky. Light glanced off mirrors and discreet touches of gilt filigree set in the wall panelling. It reminded her of some exotic sultan's palace.

He turned to face her, his lean, stern face taut and strained, his dark eyes intense. 'I had decided not to see you again,' he said abruptly.

Her heart pained, and she folded her arms over her breasts to protect herself from more wounds. Why put herself through this? 'Then why—?' She made an inarticulate gesture. Her voice came out in a dry croak. 'Why are we here?'

'You know why.' The words were wrenched from him, as if he'd had a bitter struggle with his pride, and lost. He strode across and his hands lifted as though to touch her, but he controlled them sharply and let them fall. 'Seeing you again… You know what I want. What we both want.' His deep voice was harsh.

The fire in his eyes fuelled the old yearning in her, and played on her weakness. In a confusion of emotion and resolve, she clenched her hands against her to prevent herself from throwing herself into his arms.

As though he read the conflict in her face, a flush darkened the taut, bronzed skin across his proud cheekbones, and he swung stiffly away from her, and continued his impassioned words, pacing about with a fierce, relentless dignity.

'I am—deeply remorseful to have hurt you.' He cast her a searing look from beneath his lashes. 'I'm not *altogether* heartless. I admit I didn't understand how much working at the bank meant to you. I hoped you would see that another job, in another place, would make it easy for us to—' He made an abrupt, wordless gesture and with simmering restraint, 'From your long silence, Eleanor, I gathered that with you the job was everything.' His shoulders were rigidly set, his hands bunched into fists while he waited for her reply.

Passionate, truthful words of her love and longing for him rose to her tongue, but her courage to express them failed her. Even so, as if he'd read them in her face, triumph lit the ardent gaze, and he added very softly, 'But seeing you now, I just can't believe that.'

He moved swiftly to her, his chest just a centimetre from hers. Her resolve to resist him warred with his formidable sexual power. His deep, seductive voice pulled at her with its smouldering intensity. 'You have to acknowledge that at least now there are no more barriers between us. I'm not your employer. You're not my PA. Now, we're just a man and a woman.'

The words stirred her to her depths, but her battles of the past weeks were too fresh to be dismissed. 'Sam,' she said unsteadily, shaking her head, 'it's not so easy.'

The dark flame flared in his eyes. 'Yes, it is. Don't try to deny this.' He curved his fingers under her chin and tilted up her face. His voice thickened. 'This isn't the time for us to lie to each other to save face, sweetheart. Passion isn't something you can hide.'

The endearment touched that deep inner spring she was fighting so hard to quell. Desire unfurled in her belly, and she felt the immediate, swelling heat to her breasts. She gazed into the dark eyes glinting in his proud, strong face, his mouth twisted with emotion, and the irresistible force of her love overwhelmed her.

She kissed him, and, as though it was the spark to the bonfire, he crushed her to him, and took charge, possessing her lips with scorching authority. Her body blazed like a torch, and she threw every atom of herself into his embrace with willing abandonment.

With wild, panting urgency they tore at each other's clothes, their hands barely steady in their haste to remove the constricting barriers to skin on skin. For a second he stood naked before her, in all his bronzed, muscled magnificence, feasting on her nude body with his aroused black eyes. Then he lifted her in his arms as though she were weightless, and tossed her onto his bed. He came down beside her, triumph mingling with the fire in his dark, devouring gaze.

In the first ferocious urgency, they made hot, clumsy love, rushing to a shattering climax in almost unbelievable concert. Then, long into the afternoon, while the storm raged over Sydney, with sizzling deliberation, Sam slowed passion to an infinitely more languorous pace, relishing every curve and hollow of her nude body, teasing the sweet strawberry nipples, tasting the honeyed secrets beneath her soft tangle of curls. With fierce, erotic tenderness, he roused Ellie to the wildest fever-pitch she'd ever known, until she begged for him to take her.

When he judged the moment right, he plunged into her, burying his hard shaft in her to the hilt, and pleasured her with slow, sinuous strokes, increasing the tempo into a virile, athletic rhythm that transported her beyond the pinnacle of ecstasy.

Much later, past satiety and exhaustion, she lay beside him in the huge bed, her head resting on his ribs, gazing drowsily through the domed ceiling at the midnight sky. Her body felt supple and replete.

'Tomorrow…' His deep murmur sounded sonorous against her ear. 'We'll send the car over to pick up your things.'

Ellie tensed. 'What things?'

'Everything you need. Your clothes, your books. Your music.'

She lay still for a moment, tilted her head around to look at him, then stirred herself to sit up. She pushed aside the red mass of hair tumbling over her shoulders. 'Why would we do that?'

'So you can be comfortable.' He surveyed her white naked-ness with slumbrous satisfaction, then bent his dark head to graze her bare shoulder with his lips. His mouth curved in a grin. 'I think you would miss your shoes.'

She caught her breath. 'But—I don't need them here. I live there.'

With studied casualness he said, 'I think it's better if you live here. Hornsby's too far.'

She felt stunned. For a few moments she let the dream dazzle her. Belonging to him. Sleeping in his arms every night. The intimacy of it. Everything she'd hardly dared to wish. Well, nearly everything. Pleasure, romance and…

'For—for how long does this invitation extend?' she said lightly.

His black lashes flickered down, and he hesitated. His

dark eyes connected with hers for an unreadable instant, then slid away. 'Who knows?' He shrugged, and a warning pang shot through her. 'A week, a year. Until we've had our fill of each other.'

He kissed her, stroked her hair back behind her ear, and said gruffly, 'That might take a while.' He pulled her down beside him, and gathered her against his broad, warm chest. 'We'll work out the details in the morning.'

She closed her eyes, but her mind wouldn't stop spinning. He could be hers. For a while.

A week, or a year…

A year of heavenly delights.

But after the year—what?

She had to face it, be honest with herself. He'd already shown her how ruthless he could be. How long before she was back on the scrap heap, another precious year of her life wasted, left with an incurable heartbreak?

But it was tempting. Could she do it, live the glamorous life? She would have to put aside thoughts of a child for another year or so. Then a year or two to get over him and save up again. Although after that, at thirty-three or thereabouts…

She fell off her cloud with a crash. Thirty-three was too late. Already she was in the danger zone.

She worried and churned while the moon sank low in the sky, and the starlight grew faint, then extinguished altogether. At last, in the first grey light, she carefully disentangled herself from Sam's strong, warm limbs, and slipped from the bed.

A few minutes later, a small sound impinged on his consciousness, and Sam stirred himself from his dream to a vague sense of bliss. The smile swelled in his heart in sleepy recollection. Eleanor. He reached for her.

Nothing.

He half opened his eyes. Her place was still warm. His eyes drifted shut and he drowsed, waiting for her. After a hazy time he resurfaced, and forced himself to lift his head.

Blearily he scanned the room. The shadows were shrinking into the corners, but there was no sign of her. With a sudden foreboding in his bones he got up, pulled jeans from a drawer and dragged them on.

He found her in the living room. She was fully dressed in her suit and heels, handbag slung on her shoulder, her glorious hair tamed into a neat coil in the nape of her neck. She was leaning over a table, frowning at a sheet of paper, her pen poised while she considered. She started, and straightened up when he walked in. 'Oh,' she said, her eyes widening.

Her eyelashes gave a nervous flicker, and with a lurch Sam knew. He nodded towards the paper. 'For me?'

She looked pale and drawn, her blue eyes bruised and shadowy in the pale light. Her dismay at being caught was almost tangible. 'I didn't want to wake you.'

He kept his expression under control, though he could feel an unpleasant blood-beat in his temples. 'Isn't it…?' He forced his lungs on. 'Isn't it early to be going out?'

'I'm…' She hesitated, then said, in her low voice, 'I need to go home.'

A coldness began to seep through his insides. To stall her, he tried the only thing he knew: drew her to him, kissed her cheek and the corner of her mouth. Generous girl that she was, she complied, put her arms around his neck. He crushed her to him, felt her precious heartbeat against his chest, then as the inevitable desire rose between them felt her pull back. In the empty space in his arms he felt the desolate chill of goodbye.

'But you are coming back,' he said, still careful, in the face of defeat, not to pressure her.

Her gaze wavered over him, down to his bare feet, took in his jeans and chest. Her soft mouth, still red from his kisses, made a telling little tremor. He considered seducing her back into his bed, but there was a certain nervy resolution in her posture, as of a decision reached, and he had his pride.

She brushed his bristly cheek with a gentle hand. 'Sam, I

love—love being with you. But I'm afraid I'm not really mistress material.'

Mistress material. A blade sliced through him, but he kept severe control.

Her face was working with distress. 'Last night was wonderful,' she said, regret in her warm, husky voice, blue eyes swirling with some dark tragedy. 'It would be gorgeous being here with you, but I—have goals of my own.'

'Goals.' It was difficult to smile. His heart was slamming so hard he could barely breathe, and a hoarseness entered his voice. He didn't want to sound as if he was begging, but it was necessary to point out the obvious. 'I have no intention of making your career suffer, Eleanor. I know how important it is to you. I can be of great help to you.'

She shook her head, her slim hands fluttering, as if what he'd said had somehow proven how hopeless he was.

'Look—' He felt himself flush to hear the note of desperation in his voice. 'I should have made myself clear.' As happened on the rare occasions he felt powerless, his hands flew around like some old Greek's. 'I—I fully recognise how independent you are. We'll get the lawyers to draw up a contract to protect your interests. You won't be worse off financially, far from it.'

She covered her ears in a small, defensive gesture. 'Please, Sam.' The words came out almost as a strangled cry, and she turned her face away from him.

Humiliation flooded his soul like blood.

She started for the foyer. Dimly he knew he'd said all the wrong things, but what were the right ones? With women, a man never knew.

'I'll drive you,' he said quickly, catching up with her, thinking of the long drive there. Plenty of time to talk her round.

'No. No, please,' she said, stepping into the lift. 'I've phoned for a taxi.' She turned to face him. 'It's better this way.' That fragile pulse was beating in her throat. He stared, unbelieving, as tears filled her eyes. 'Goodbye, Sam.'

A crippling pain inhabited his being. For a crazed instant he teetered on the verge of spilling his guts. Pleading, like some love-struck teenager.

Instead, he controlled himself in time and stood back with the dignity of a man. His face felt stiff, and when the words came he knew they sounded cold and formal. 'I wish you well on your climb to the top, Eleanor.'

CHAPTER ELEVEN

How the rich lived.

There was no need to phone for a taxi. Irene said she would pick Ellie up on the way to the airport, and at the appointed time a limo drew up at her door. A uniformed chauffeur sprang out to help her with her bag, and she was ushered to join Irene in its plush interior like Princess Mary.

It was clear now why Irene had seemed vague about reservations. The Stilakos family didn't make reservations. They had their own private jet.

She might have enjoyed it all more if she hadn't felt like such an imposter. Irene had wanted her on the basis of her being connected to her son, and now the connection was broken. Should she explain, or did Irene know? she wondered, eyeing the bright-eyed older woman after they'd greeted each other with a warm hug.

It didn't take long for the sore point to come up. They were in the sky, with Sydney passing beneath them like a sequinned cloth. 'What will Sam do without you?' Irene said. A gleam of satisfaction lit the older woman's eyes every time they settled on her. 'It will do him so much good to miss you.'

Ellie felt the heat in her cheeks. The choking pain threatened to burst through her chest. 'Well, no. Actually I don't work for Sam now. I've got another job.' The words sounded so suspect, even to her own ears, she wasn't surprised when Irene arched her brows and looked keenly at her through her specs.

'I felt I needed to extend myself,' she explained. 'It's time to set my goals in place and carve my path to the top. I'm a career girl, you know, Irene. Through and through.'

Irene looked doubtful, and Ellie felt a spurt of exasperation. What would it take to convince this old woman?

'Oh, sure I liked my job at the bank,' she went on breezily. 'I'd been there a long time. Personal connections are all very well, but, between you and me, nothing can measure up to the thrill of discovering what you're capable of in the world of big business and testing your abilities to the limit. That's the real adrenaline rush.' The scepticism in the shrewd grey eyes only increased, and she added firmly, 'I've joined a team of management consultants.'

Irene's musing, 'Oh-h-h. Is that right?' was unsettling. Ellie could practically see her well-exercised brain-cells ticking into calculation.

Lunch was served by a uniformed flight attendant, but Ellie couldn't eat a thing. People who'd ruined their own lives had no need of sustenance. They lived on their regrets. She hadn't even been able to raise a laugh at the postcard she'd received from Tierra del Fuego. 'On my way home to you, babe. Sorry the team was held up. Love, Mark.'

Love. Ironic that. It was a word he'd carefully avoided in the past. That blonde in Melbourne must have taught him a thing or two.

The sight of sea and long white sandy beaches should have lifted her spirits. As the plane circled Coolangatta Airport before coming in to land, the famous strip of high-rises shimmered in the sun with the old promise of holidays and pleasure.

Funny how the idea of pleasure could be so depressing.

An elderly couple wearing expensive-looking casuals and anxious expressions stood waiting in the arrivals lounge. When she and Irene walked in, there was a moment of mutual hesitation, then the couple and Irene surged forward to fall on each other's necks with teary sobs. In a storm of questions and pro-testations and more hugs, all three of them talked so fast no one could possibly make sense of anything anyone else said.

After they'd mopped up, Irene introduced them to Ellie as her brother Jack, and his wife Rosemary, explaining they were the groom's parents. 'And this is Ellie,' Irene said with a warm look at Ellie, 'a friend of Sam's.'

Jack's and Rosemary's brows shot up and they looked Ellie over with surmise. Ellie fired a questioning frown at Irene and was met with an innocent smile. Was there the faintest tinge of smugness in that smile? Ellie wondered.

The flight crew appeared with their baggage, then handed it over to a waiting chauffeur. With a minimum of fuss they were soon in another limo, cutting a swathe through the Gold Coast traffic.

'How are the preparations coming?' Irene enquired.

The couple looked at each other and Jack rolled his eyes. Rosemary inclined her head. Scarcely moving her mouth, she said, 'They've been problems.' She gave Irene a speaking look. 'I think you can guess.'

'Ah.' Irene narrowed her eyes and nodded. 'Yes, I think I can.' She slanted Ellie a meaningful glance.

'Luckily our villa is away from all the goings-on.' Rosemary's lips thinned. 'I hope you two won't mind being in the thick of it. We're hosting the groom's dinner tonight at the Palazzo, so fingers crossed.'

The Palazzo Versace was as elegant as its brochures promised. The resort was lapped by the ocean Broadwater. From where Ellie stood in the white-and-gold marbled vesti-bule, her view across its green lagoon seemed faintly reminis-cent of Venice, but a gleaming, sprucified Venice, a Venice that was still gracious, but reassuringly solid.

Theirs was not the only limo to draw up to its charming entrance. As Ellie smoothed down her slim dress more cars arrived, disgorging more glittering guests. Some she recognised from the television world, while others bore the faintly bored, relaxed demeanour of the very rich.

A noisy group were in occupation of the bar at one end of the lobby. Ellie's experienced eye could tell they were already into party mode. They kept shouting with laughter, and welcoming every new arrival with theatrical embraces and much witty repartee.

While Irene dealt with Reception, Rosemary and Jack made beckoning motions to someone in the bar crowd. A slight, intense-looking man detached himself from the group he was with, and tried to snag the attention of a vivacious young woman in the throes of relating some story to her friends. She was telling her story with gusto, throwing her arms about and screaming with laughter.

Natalie Stilakos.

Who else would flaunt hectares of her naked midriff between a couple of scraps of floaty gauze to her fiancé's family?

The black-rooted blonde spun about, and as her glance homed in on her in-laws, past and future, the laughter died on her face, to be reconstituted into a nervous, unconvincing smirk. She clutched her fiancé's arm, and it seemed to Ellie that the couple braced themselves. They started across the foyer, Natalie clinging tight to her lover's arm.

Michael composed his rather sallow face into a smile, and greeted his aunt with a few stilted, though friendly, words and a quick kiss, and Natalie was forced to follow suit, though her lips made no actual skin contact.

'It's so nice to see you, Natalie,' Irene said warmly. 'Welcome again to the family, dear. I'm sure you'll make Michael a lovely wife.'

Natalie's smile faded. Her black eyes glowered through the heavy kohl smudging their rims. 'What's that supposed to mean?'

Rosemary and Jack made nervous shuffling movements and pretended to look out at the lagoon. Michael quickly took his fiancée's wrist and gave it a little shake. 'Chill, darling,' he said, winking and giving everyone a grin. 'Wedding nerves. It'll all be over soon.' Everyone joined in the false hearty laugh.

Rosemary quickly eased the moment on, announcing, to Ellie's intense chagrin, 'And this is Ellie, Sam's girlfriend.'

Ellie would have denied it but for a sudden steel clamp on her elbow. No wonder Sam had such a strong grip.

She managed a smile and accepted Michael's hand. He examined her with frank curiosity, then leaned forward to peck her cheek as if she were family. Still with her smile in place, she turned to Natalie. After an awkward second, the blonde stuck out a hand for a brief brushing of fingers, her eyes guarded. 'But aren't you Sam's receptionist?'

'Oh, no, no,' Irene intervened before Ellie had a chance to speak. 'Ellie's a management consultant.' She gave a fond laugh. 'Sam gets all the benefit of her advice at home.'

Ellie swivelled an outraged look at Irene, who bestowed such an affectionate beam on her it was all she could do not to gasp.

A porter stood patiently by waiting to escort them to the condominium owned by the Stilakos family. Rosemary and Jack made moves to leave, with an arrangement to meet later, and to Ellie's relief the group broke up. Michael called after Ellie with an invitation to come back down once she was settled. The glance the bride flung Ellie over her shoulder was puzzled.

The Principessa Suite was spacious and filled with light, its gleaming marble floors exquisitely tiled with a mosaic design. Broad balcony windows opened to views of the Broadwater. Ellie barely gave herself a chance to take in the fabulous Versace furnishings, before advancing on Sam's mother, who was narrowly inspecting the master suite.

'What are you up to, Irene?' Ellie's hands were on her hips. 'What's the idea of telling people I'm Sam's girlfriend?'

'Oh-h-h...' Irene shuddered '...wasn't it harrowing?' Kicking off her shoes, she flopped onto a sumptuous king-sized bed, draped in the rich deep colours of the Renaissance, and gave a throaty chuckle. 'Did you see Natalie's face?'

'I could hardly miss. Why did you do it?'

Irene sat back up, all wide-eyed innocence. '*I* didn't say you were his girlfriend. It was Rosemary who said that.' She gave her head a despairing shake at Rosemary's chronic hopelessness. 'Trust her to leap to conclusions.' With a sigh she sank back on the assortment of tasselled cushions and pillows adorning the bed.

Ellie checked her retort and drew a deep, calming breath. 'You could have corrected her impression, though, couldn't you? You didn't have to encourage it.'

Irene arranged herself more comfortably, and cast Ellie an amused glance. 'Oh, don't give me that stern face. I get enough of that from Sam. Why can't you go along with it for a couple of days? It will serve that little piece right for letting people think Sam can't get over her. ' She leaned up on a gold and purple embroidered cushion and her eyes glistened. 'It would be better if he was here with you, of course. Why don't I give him a call and tell him you've broken your ankle?'

Ellie shook her head in bemusement. 'What are you talking about? Sam wouldn't… Don't, please, for heaven's *sake*!' She flushed. Her feelings about Sam and the things that had happened between them were raw. Too raw to be used in some game. With difficulty she said, 'I don't think you realise, Irene, how—how painful and embarrassing this would be for me if Sam found out. He was my boss, you know.'

'But he isn't now, is he? *Is* he, Ellie? It's a whole new ball game.'

Ellie's body suddenly felt twitchy and in need of fast, furious exercise. She walked out into the sitting room and back again, her hands as restless as her feet.

'Anyway,' she said, ignoring Irene's sly riposte, 'why should Natalie care what Sam does? They're divorced, aren't they? She doesn't have any hold on Sam. She's marrying someone else, for goodness' sake. She and Sam are—over.' She stopped to gaze out at the Broadwater, but all she could see was what she couldn't stop seeing. Sam's dark eyes, aflame for *her*. She turned to Irene and said in a choked voice, 'Aren't they?'

Irene was watching her from her room with a shrewd little smile. 'Of course they are. They've been over practically since the first.'

'Really?'

Irene gave her a long look and heaved a sigh. 'Yes, yes, yes. The whole thing was a mistake. I doubt if he'd have stayed married to her for as long as he did if it hadn't been for the baby.'

Ellie's eyes sprang wide with shock. 'They have a child?'

Irene compressed her lips. 'No, but I'm pretty sure there was one. I can usually tell when a girl's in the family way.' Her eyes clouded and she shook her head. 'I'm afraid the baby didn't eventuate. Goodness knows what happened. Whatever it was, things went very wrong between them. Sam would never breathe a word about it, of course. Then five minutes after the wedding Natalie was flaunting her affair with Michael, and the marriage was doomed.' She sighed and patted her cushion. 'To give the girl her due, she's tried everything she could think of to persuade Sam and Michael to patch things up. If Sam would only get over it and come to the wedding…' She lay back and lapsed into gloomy thought.

Ellie stood very still and forced herself to say coolly, 'I suppose it would be hard for Sam to watch his wife marry someone else.'

'Oh…!' Irene roused herself to make a dismissive sweep of her hand. 'The spoilt hussy barely was his wife. But Sam's an old-fashioned Greek man at heart. He's too much like his father. If he believes his honour has been insulted he can be very proud.' She rolled her eyes. '*Men*. Who knows how the creatures think?' With another hefty sigh, she rolled back on her pillows and stared at the ornate baroque ceiling.

Ellie went to her own room, which was as richly furnished

as Irene's. Mirrors and sparkling Italian mosaics reflected the
watery light from the lagoon, but it was hard to appreciate it
all when her heart knew only darkness.

Would rejecting a Greek man three times constitute an insult
to his honour? she wondered. Of course it would. It would sting
any man like fury. He'd never want to lay eyes on her again.

But there was no use giving in to this dreadful, tearing
ache. Wishing she'd taken a chance. Tears swelled her throat.
Hoping…*pretending* love had happened to her too, the way
she had with Mark. It was ironic really, how she'd thought
she'd come to terms with all this ages ago. But the same old
conditions still seemed to apply. For Ellie O'Dea, no love at
all was better than half-love. So even if she loved Sam enough
for ten people…

'Ellie?'

She pulled herself together. Irene had resettled herself on a
chaise longue in the sitting room and was riffling through her
handbag. When she saw Ellie she pushed the bag aside and
threw up her hands. 'Oh, all right. I give in. Tell them all the
truth about you and Sam if you have to. I'm sorry if you were
embarrassed. I suppose I hoped you might be a woman after
my own heart.' She placed a be-ringed hand over her breast and
gazed at Ellie, her grey eyes sparkling with reproach. 'I had the
impression you might enjoy a little graceful subterfuge. It never
occurred to me you might actually *be* a goody-two-shoes.'

Ellie gasped and let out a shocked laugh. 'Irene. You are
the limit!'

The older woman grinned. 'I sincerely hope so. Now be a
dear, will you, and phone for some tea? And ask them to send
up a butler.'

'A butler?'

She elevated her brows. 'Well, dear, we need to unpack.
Someone has to locate my pills.'

Remorse snapped Ellie from her gloom. What could she be
thinking of, ticking off an old woman with a heart problem?

'Yes, yes, of course,' she said, moving across to pick up the phone. 'And why don't you have a little rest afterwards so you'll feel nice and fresh to meet Rosemary and Jack?'

'Good idea.' Irene's eyes twinkled. 'I think I might need to be fresh. What about you?'

Ellie shook her head. She was restless, and she wasn't especially hungry. No, Ellie O'Dea, for all her faults, was an action woman. It was time to brave the bride.

Once the butler was ensconced and Irene was settled with some delicious pastries from the Palazzo kitchen and a fat romance novel, Ellie slipped into her room to change.

The party had dispersed a little in the time she'd been away. People had drifted out to the lagoon terrace. Natalie was still near the bar, hunched in an armchair, scowling morosely into space. Michael was engaged in urgent conversation with an actressy-looking brunette who kept glaring around him at Natalie, in between bouts of furious hissing and ferocious gestures with her fist.

Not a good time, Ellie's antennae suggested.

She paused for a moment to decide where best to head, and a waiter materialised beside her. She ordered a squash and sauntered through the glass doors to the terrace. At once she was assailed with the holiday smells of swimming pools, sunscreen and salt sea air.

An umbrella table was vacant at the edge of the party set, and in no time a tall glass garnished with lemon was misting with condensation in front of her. She paid and smiled her thanks, then settled in to watch the human drama.

Across the lagoon on the beach side, people—couples mainly—lolled side by side on loungers, reading or dozing in casual intimacy. Occasionally they'd disturb themselves to apply lotion to each other's glistening bodies, or drink from each other's glasses. They'd murmur things into each other's ears, and writhe with sexy laughter at their private little secrets.

Other people romped with their children in the turquoise waters. Happy people. People with love in their lives.

A shadow blocked out the sun, and she looked up. Natalie hovered there, a couple of splotches on her pretty make-up job that looked suspiciously as if she'd been having a weep.

'Are you and Sam really together?' She remained standing for a second, then pulled over a chair and sat down. Like a genie, the waiter appeared from nowhere and she ordered a margarita.

'No,' Ellie admitted.

'Oh, right.' Natalie's gaze clouded. 'I thought Irene must have been winding me up. I lived with Sam long enough to know that much about him. He'd never sleep with his office girl, unless he's changed a whole lot. As soon as any of them showed they thought he was hot…' She grimaced and made a slashing motion across her throat. 'You're his receptionist, aren't you?'

'I was his Personal Assistant.'

'*Was!*' Her dark eyes widened. 'You don't mean he got rid of you, too?'

The raw spot must have grown its first delicate protective layer, for Ellie found herself able to say quite calmly, 'Yes, I'm afraid he did.' She took a long, sustained sip of her squash.

The bottle-blonde studied her, unexpected sympathy infusing her smudgy gaze. 'Oh. Oh, that's a shame.' She ran a pensive finger around the rim of her glass. 'But you must be still in there with a chance, or why has Irene brought you?'

Ellie shrugged. 'Oh, well, this arrangement was made a while ago. You know…before…' She echoed Natalie's throat-cutting gesture.

Natalie nodded her understanding, resting her head in her hands and staring gloomily at the table-top while she toyed with a coaster. 'I was hoping there might still be a chance of him turning up,' she said casually. 'If you two *had* been together, I thought you might've been able to talk him into it. I know he has all these really old-fashioned *ideas*, and he never forgives a person for *anything*, but it would mean so much to Michael if he would just get over it and—move on.' She shook her ragged head and chewed her lip.

Ellie stirred her ice cubes with the straw, wondering how long it took the average man to get over a divorce. Four years should have been long enough, surely. When would Sam get over it? What was wrong with him?

Natalie had lapsed into a frowning reverie, and in an effort to distract her Ellie hazarded, 'You aren't having a hen-party? You've already had it?'

She looked up, then her dark eyes shifted to evade Ellie's. 'Oh, look, who needs one? I can do without people who have to turn every little thing a person says or does into a major Cecil B De Mille production. What do I care? All I want is to marry the love of my life on that beach tomorrow and forget about the world. I don't need anyone to hold up my train.' She flung out her hands. 'It's a beach, for God's sake.'

Ellie wondered if the brunette in the bar had been a bridesmaid.

Natalie finished her drink and rose. She made a move to leave, then turned back and bent towards Ellie. 'You know,' she said abruptly, 'Sam is really an old-fashioned Greek man, at heart, like his dad. And like mine. He doesn't understand that a woman might want to have a *life*. He thinks a woman should be *this*, or should be *that*, but she can't be both. What he wants is someone who's happy to be a good little wife and mother.' She turned away again, lifting a casual hand in farewell. 'See you.'

Ellie smiled, though an amusing irony was crushing her heart. Maybe that *was* what he'd wanted. At least, that was what he'd wanted with Natalie. He wanted a whole different ball game with his ex-PA.

The blonde sashayed away. Just what was it that made some women so desirable as wives that men would fight over them and move heaven and earth to win them, while others could only ever aspire to being mistresses or live-in housekeepers?

Was it their clothes, their hair, their beauty? Their wit? Their senses of humour? And if Irene had been right about the baby, what was the tragedy that had driven the newly-weds apart instead of drawing them closer? She could just imagine Sam with a baby.

Suddenly the smell of sunscreen and swimming pool was too festive for Ellie's mood. She dragged herself up and headed inside for the lifts. Why had she agreed to come to a wedding, of all things? Weddings were only enjoyable to people who'd successfully had one, or people who had every chance of pulling one off.

A lift arrived almost immediately. The doors slid open to reveal it chock-a-block with Irene, the butler and all her baggage.

'Oh, Ellie. Good, good,' she said, bustling out. 'I'm glad I've caught you.'

'What's happening?' Ellie said, surprised. 'Are we leaving?'

'No.' Irene explained that Rosemary and Jack simply wanted her to stay over in their villa so they could catch up properly. 'You come if you want to, Ellie.'

'I think I might stay here,' she said, sensing she would be an intruder in the family reunion. 'I'll see you all at the dinner.'

She noticed that Irene didn't try to insist. In fact, she looked quite excited, as if she had some elderly mischief up her sleeve.

Ellie followed the small entourage to the hotel entrance, and watched the butler and Jack's chauffeur bundle Irene and her belongings into the limo. She felt a twinge of misgiving. Wasn't she supposed to keep her eye on Irene?

A tinted window slid down in the rear and Irene put her head out. 'Mind you have a good time, now,' she warned before she was swept away.

How? Ellie thought with a flat feeling. What was there for a single woman to do, alone at the Palazzo Versace?

CHAPTER TWELVE

THERE were changes in the Principessa. The bed in the master suite looked as if it had been stripped and remade with fresh linen, and Ellie's clothes had been hung there, her toiletries arrayed in the bathroom.

Someone—Irene's butler, she presumed—had been busy.

Should she indulge herself by wallowing in that enormous spa bath before it was time to change for dinner?

While the tub filled she undressed in the steamy atmosphere, then caught up her hair in a clip. Over the gushing water, she heard what could have been a knock. Probably another maid with towels. She turned off the taps and slipped on a luxurious Versace bathrobe. The knock came again, strong and unequivocal. Hang on, she frowned, tying the belt around her as she padded across the marble floors in her bare feet.

She opened the door and her heart jolted in shock and an immediate deep, wild joy there was no repressing. Sam stood there, tall, dark and solidly real, his dark eyes glinting in instant connection with hers.

His lean, powerful form was encased in close-fitting jeans and a black tee shirt that outlined the contours of his chest, and clung to his arms and shoulders. The sheer sexual impact of seeing his bare arms again, bronzed, muscular and so close, trapped the breath in her throat.

His brilliant dark gaze ran over her state of dishabille as

though her robe were transparent. Overwhelmingly reminded of the hungry, panting creature he'd reduced her to in those sinewy arms with such ease only a couple of days before, she had to restrain herself from stepping into his embrace.

Then the painful knowledge of the wounds they'd inflicted on each other reasserted itself, and she drew back. The gulf between them loomed deeper than the Tasman.

'Am I allowed in?' There was a dark shadow of beard on his jaw and upper lip. The lines around his mouth were grim, and seemed more deeply etched.

She flushed. 'Of course. Please. Please do come in.' She fell back to allow him past, and her glance fell on the suitcase he was towing.

He parked it inside the door, strolled through into the sitting room and turned to appraise her. Their last goodbye hung heavy on the air, though his eyes were cool and steady.

Her hand strayed to her hair. She saw his glance and knew the nervous gesture had betrayed her. 'I—I wasn't expecting you.'

'I can see that. I'm sorry if I've arrived at an inconvenient time. I don't mean to upset you.' The quiet, dry tones of his voice wrung her insides.

'I'm not upset,' she retorted quickly.

He searched her face with a veiled gaze, then glanced about, through the open door to the bedroom where her undergarments were laid out on the bed. 'Are we alone here?'

She nodded. As though more layers of clothing could hide her vulnerable feelings, she wished fervently she had the underwear *on*. Her hand crept to draw the lapels of her robe together at the neck.

His sharp glance caught the movement, and her feeling of being at a disadvantage deepened. His brows edged up. 'Mind if I ask what you've done with my mother?'

She explained about Irene's departure, adding, 'I'm meeting them all a little later at the groom's dinner.'

The space between them throbbed with her aching awareness of her love for him. He was so straight and tall and handsome, so intelligent and honest and stirringly sexy. If he took her in his arms now…

Indecision flooded her heart. What if she changed her mind? He was here. Might there be a chance he'd come because he still wanted her? If she agreed to be with him on his terms, it would ease this cruel yearning, at least in the short term. The more she thought of it, the more it seemed obvious that he *was* here for her. Who else?

She swallowed. 'Are you—? Do you…? Have—have you come to see Irene?'

He met her eyes coolly. 'Why else but to pay my respects to the bride and groom?' There was no softening of his expression, and her small hope died.

He strolled over to pick up his suitcase, then paused. 'Would it embarrass you if we were to go to this thing together?'

Her heart gave a wild flutter. 'Oh. No. Not at all. Where—where are you staying?'

'I'll take a room in the hotel.'

Regret washed through her for the constraint between them now. 'Oh, Sam. Is that really necessary? This *is* your apartment. There's plenty of room.'

He looked down, then raised his glinting gaze to her. A grim little smile twisted his mouth. 'It is necessary, believe me.' He strolled to the door with his athletic, long-limbed stride, and every one of his steps tore at her with their finality. He paused with his hand on the doorknob. 'I'll call for you. At seven?'

She nodded, unable to speak because of the tide of disappointment rising to engulf her. The door clicked shut behind him. Nothing could have stated more clearly the impossibility of reneging on a rejection delivered three times to a proud man.

It was too late to change her mind.

She hauled herself miserably back to the bathroom and sank into the bubbles. At least she would have this one last evening with him. She made the stern resolve to conquer her grief and savour every precious last moment of his company.

Her wardrobe hadn't offered much choice, so for the dinner she'd decided to resort to Flirty Noir. In truth, she'd gone off it since that last fateful day at work, remembering how Sam had criticised it as inappropriate. She had an anxious moment wondering if he would remember it, then persuaded herself he wouldn't. What man ever remembered what a woman wore?

Still, with the most desirable man in Australia as her date, it did feel like an occasion worth some trouble. She rose from the bubbles and towelled herself dry. Despite everything, she did feel the tiniest glow of anticipation. Perhaps Sam would thaw out as the evening progressed. Perhaps they could recover some sort of ease with each other.

When she had the dress on, it still had the old magic. Her breasts were as full and perky, their swell just as defined through the embroidered black tulle. It was pleasing, she thought, turning sideways in front of the mirror. Perhaps even a little cheering.

She applied her make-up with special care, and didn't spare the eye-shadow.

She heard Sam arrive, and called out to him to let himself in and help himself to a drink. When she'd brushed her hair into a gleaming river, she squirted a cloud of perfume into the air, walked through it, and on a deep, quivering breath opened the bedroom doors.

Faint masculine scents of soap and sandalwood reached her. Sam was seated on a sofa, one arm resting on his thigh in the classic masculine pose as he frowningly perused some papers. He looked elegant, in a black evening suit and open-necked white shirt. His blue-black hair was still damp, his lean, tanned jaw smooth-shaven. He was so darkly gorgeous her heart surged with longing.

At the sound of the doors he glanced up. His black eyes flared into riveted focus, then made a slow, scorchingly sensual sweep of her from head to toe. For a few thundering moments the tempestuous passions of her last day in his office were potently present.

All at once she felt breathless, overwhelmingly conscious of the simmering desire snapping the air between them like an electric arc. Desire, she recalled now with a sudden lurch, that had been tinged with disdain. She felt an agonised doubt about her appearance. Did he think she looked like a tart now? What if he was embarrassed by her before his entire family? Red-hot humiliation threatened to surface, and she said stiffly, 'Do I—does it look all right? Do you think it's—suitable?'

He rose to his feet. Something flickered in his dark, impenetrable gaze as he looked at her. 'It's perfect,' he said softly. 'You've never looked more beautiful.'

Such unexpected generosity after the jagged emotions of their last goodbye pierced her heart, and her throat thickened.

His brows drew together and he looked keenly at her, and held out his hand for hers. 'Come on, then. Let's go and surprise them.' She made a constrained movement, but their fingers didn't quite touch.

Though thronging with billionaires and celebrities, the dinner was an informal affair.

There was a reception area outside the silk-panelled ballroom where Jack and Rosemary greeted their guests. The large crowd of family and friends were being served drinks and hors d'oeuvres. Some of the guests had wandered inside, where tables had been set around a sumptuous buffet, laden with delicacies. A few of the younger people were already on the dance floor.

When Ellie walked in with Sam, the first person she spotted was his mother. Irene appeared to be in sparkling spirits. She was holding a glass and laughing about something with Jack, while next to them Rosemary stood, deep in conversation with a middle-aged Greek couple. Natalie's parents? Ellie wondered.

Rosemary glanced their way and her eyes slid back in a double take. She leaned over to Jack and murmured something out of the corner of her mouth. Jack's head snapped back, and his bristly grey eyebrows swooped up in astonishment. 'Sam!'

At least ninety heads turned, in varying degrees of surprise and curiosity. After an uncertain pause, in which urgent, meaningful glances were telegraphed from woman to woman across the room, Jack surged forward with his arms outstretched. '*Sam*, my boy.'

It was the signal.

'Sam.'

'*Sam!*'

People came from all corners to welcome Sam. Ellie stood back while he was embraced, exclaimed over and had his back warmly slapped by relatives and friends, past and present. After the initial excited flurry, Sam turned his dark, inscrutable gaze on her, and with every appearance of pride drew her forward.

To her horror Rosemary burbled, 'Oh, yes, Sam, dear. We mustn't forget your lovely new fiancée.'

Mortification shocked through Ellie in a crimson tide. As though oblivious of the bombshell, Sam continued introducing her with suave aplomb. How would she explain? It would look as though she'd told people they were engaged. How did a woman inform a man that his mother was a mischief-maker?

Her frantic inner turmoil of possible explanations was interrupted when she felt someone's gaze burning a hole through her skull. She turned her head. Irene stood to one side, her hands demurely folded, the picture of a sweet elderly lady, but her eyes were dancing, pure wickedness pouring from her every blood vessel. Ellie glared at her, and the old she-devil responded with a gleeful wink.

Natalie's parents had retreated, stiff-faced, into a corner, but Sam strolled to greet them with the smooth courtesy he was master of. Natalie's father rose to the occasion with a formal, dignified, very Greek embrace, while her mother murmured some wary, indecipherable words. Ellie was just exchanging greetings with them herself when Natalie bowled in from the ballroom, Michael in tow. She stopped short, shrieked, 'Sam!' then covered her mouth with her hand.

The entire room held its breath. Incredibly, Natalie pulled herself together, seized her fiancé's hand and walked across to them with queenly dignity.

Ellie had to hand it to her. That soap Natalie was contracted to was way beneath her capabilities. Her award-winning performance enabled the greetings on both sides to go smoothly, Sam shaking his cousin Michael's hand with cool civility, even if it was tight-lipped and a little stiff.

The families then seemed to heave a sigh of relief. People started moving into the dining room and seating themselves. Irene murmured a few words to her son and went to join the oldies, while Sam steered Ellie to a table where some of his well-heeled yachting cronies were ensconced with their wives and girlfriends.

Champagne was poured, but Ellie felt it best to keep a clear head. In her dangerously emotional state, who knew what she might do to disgrace herself? The crowd converged on the buffet, and she and Sam followed, and allowed their plates to be piled with lobster and exotic salads.

Natalie came up behind Ellie at the buffet and whispered, 'You lied.'

'No, I didn't,' Ellie murmured from the corner of her mouth. 'It's a mistake. Honestly.'

'Be careful,' the blonde warned.

'What was that about?' Sam asked, frowning, when Natalie had darted away and they were back in their seats.

'Oh.' Ellie blushed, weighing up how to broach the excruciating subject. She met his questioning gaze, took a deep breath and plunged in. 'Er—she was enquiring about that vicious rumour. You know, the idea your aunt seems to have.' Sam's eyes sharpened on her face in just the way they used to when she was justifying something she'd done at work. 'I don't know how Rosemary came to think it. I'm so embarrassed, Sam. Honestly. I was mortified when I heard her say that.'

'Were you?' He studied her face with a narrow, meditative gaze.

She suffered the most frightful suspicion that Sam thought she'd done it on purpose to plant the suggestion in his head. 'Well, yes,' she said urgently, imploring him with her eyes to understand that *this* time she was speaking nothing but the unvarnished truth. 'I honestly was. I hope you don't think *I* had anything to do with it. It wasn't my doing. I've no idea where it came from, only Rosemary and Jack seemed to get the idea, and now everyone…'

Sam's thick black brows made an ominous merger. 'Is the idea *so* distasteful to you? Would you like me to make a public announcement?'

She stared at him in confusion. 'Well, no, no. It's not distasteful to *me*! I thought it would be to you.'

He sighed, and glanced irritably about at the other guests at their table. 'Look, haven't you had enough of all this yet? Can't we leave?'

They'd barely embarked on their meals. 'What, *now*?' She gave him an incredulous look, then around the brilliant room at all the people. If they left now her last evening with him would be over. He'd go off somewhere, she'd be all alone in her room… 'We can't leave yet,' she whispered.

Was he so desperate to escape? She'd been so thrilled to have him with her. Couldn't he put up with the party if she was with him? A lump rose in her throat. She stared blindly at her poor dismembered lobster for a while, then, in need of a sanctuary to compose herself, excused herself at the first opportunity and made for the bathroom.

Natalie was in there, nervily dragging quick heavy puffs from a cigarette. Judging by the density of the fumes it wasn't the first. The toxic smell made Ellie feel sick and she backed outside again and stood in the corridor, fanning herself with her hand and trying to fill her lungs with oxygen to dispel the clammy feeling.

The door opened and Natalie came out. For a woman about to walk down Paradise Beach with the love of her life, she looked strung out, her dark eyes stormy and intense.

'I don't know how you got him here, 'she said urgently to Ellie, 'but thanks.'

'It wasn't me.' Ellie shrugged. 'I don't know what inspired him to come.'

Natalie looked sceptical. 'Oh, come off it, Ellie.' She glanced about and edged a little closer. 'See if you can get him to talk to Michael.' She grabbed Ellie's arm in a desperate appeal. *'Please.'* To Ellie's horror she burst into tears.

'Oh, God.' Ellie gave a swift look around, then put her arm around Natalie's heaving shoulders and bundled her back into the Ladies. 'Here.' She shoved her a handful of tissues, and patted her back until the storm subsided.

When Natalie had blown her nose and had more of a grip, Ellie went to the door and waved it back and forth to help the fumes diminish. Thank heavens the bathroom had a super-efficient exhaust system.

'Weddings are supposed to be stressful,' Ellie said sympathetically. 'Is there anything I can do to help?'

'It's all going wrong,' Natalie squawked in her high-pitched wail. *'Again.'*

The floodgates reopened. Ellie thoughtfully closed the door and clicked the lock.

The bride dabbed at her nose with a tissue. 'Jen was supposed to be the Matron of Honour and Mad was the bridesmaid. Mad's gone off in a huff, Jen's gone home sick and Michael and I have had a fight. And I thought it was bad the *first* time.'

She gave Ellie an anguished glance through her wet mascara, and Ellie felt a wave of compassion. 'We've got all these people coming from all over.' She made vague sweeping motions. 'Athens, Italy, LA.' She put her face in her hands and rocked back and forwards on her heels. 'It was m-meant to be so beautiful. Now there won't even be a wedding party. There'll hardly be a *wedding*.'

'Don't you have a cousin or someone who can stand in for the bridesmaid?'

'Too fat,' she wept. 'All too fat.' Her nose started to run and Ellie swiftly thrust her more tissues.

Ellie sighed, and sat down on the nearest toilet seat. 'Does it matter so much if your bridesmaid is a little overweight?'

'It's the dress,' Natalie replied when the flow had stemmed a little. 'Mad's really skinny. The theme is Pisces, because that's both mine and Michael's star sign, so it has to be tight.' She glanced earnestly at Ellie. 'You know, fish scales.' Her voice veered up into her upper register. 'And now Michael will think that's my fault too.'

'The fish scales?'

'That I can't even get anyone to be my bridesmaid.' The tears started again. 'That's how it'll *look*.'

'Unless you find someone,' Ellie suggested. 'What about Michael's family?'

'They hate me. They *all* hate me. They all blame me for Sam and Michael being enemies now and…' She buried her face in her hands and sobbed. After a minute she lifted her head. Her reddened eyes slewed over Ellie and brightened a little. 'You could probably wear it if it weren't for your bust. I could get someone to work on it.'

'Oh,' Ellie said, alarmed. 'I don't think so. I don't think Sam would—'

'Sam, Sam. Always *Sam*.' As if driven stark raving mad, Natalie grabbed a couple of fistfuls of her blonde hair and made savage wrenching motions. Ellie noticed, though, that she was quite careful not to cause it any lasting disruptions. 'As soon as Sam appears everyone forgets Michael even exists. It's just Sam, Sam, Sam. He ruined my first wedding, and now he's ruining this one.'

'But you wanted him to come,' Ellie pointed out gently.

She rolled her eyes. 'Are you insane? Do you ever listen? Not for *me*. For Michael. Please, Ellie, *tell* me, will you look at the dress?'

Ellie heaved a sigh and got up. 'All right. I'll look at it. But I'd have to try it on. You can show me later.' She added firmly, 'No promises, now.'

Natalie was so pathetically grateful, Ellie felt remorse for her reluctance. But fish scales? Did a woman want to be seen by the love of her life, for what was probably the last time ever, dressed as a fish? Inevitably, her eyes misted over. She had hoped they could leave each other at the end with dignity, at least.

Outside in the corridor she was surprised to see Michael, leaning against the wall with his arms folded across his chest, scowling. He looked up anxiously, and she smiled and reassured him that Natalie was just coming. The brief exchange was interrupted by Sam, who strode up to them wearing the stern, inscrutable expression that terrified people at the bank. He directed a cold glance at his cousin, then examined her closely and muttered, 'Are you all right?'

She looked curiously from him to Michael. 'Fine. I've just been talking to Natalie. I haven't been gone that long, have I?' She gave him a searching glance. 'Were you worried?'

'Why would I be worried, Eleanor?' He turned his back on his cousin, took her arm and smoothly hustled her away from the infected zone. 'I don't think you should allow yourself to get too friendly with people like that.'

'Oh, Sam. They aren't so bad. I know Natalie's your ex, and no one likes their ex, but…' She met his chilly glance and bit her lip. 'Sorry.'

In fact, an idea had occurred to her inside that toilet cubicle while Natalie was going through meltdown. For all her drama, there was something quite vulnerable and endearing about the shaggy-haired blonde. Was this why Sam had fallen in love with her? Why he'd wanted to *marry* her?

A horrifying possibility began to unfurl its poisonous tentacles. She'd shied away from imagining him with Natalie because it cut her like hot knives. But now she couldn't stop imagining it. What if he was still in love with her? Was this the answer?

She supposed bitterly that he needed a woman who could bring out his protective instincts. Underneath all that smooth, sophisticated intelligence, he was still just a macho male animal. A together woman like herself, renowned for her independence and efficiency, could never have filled the bill.

'What's wrong?' Sam halted her to scrutinise her face. 'You're looking a bit peaky. I've noticed you've hardly eaten anything yet. I think you should finish your dinner, then go back upstairs and lie down.'

'Oh, thanks.' She knew he was raw over her not agreeing to be his mistress, but did he have to be so unflattering? It was as though he couldn't wait now to unload her. She decided to put an end to her misery, and know the worst, once and for all. 'As a matter of fact,' she said casually, 'I was just thinking…I can see why you fell in love with Natalie.'

His brows shot up, then he gazed at her for a long time, a frown gathering in his brilliant black eyes. 'Who said I was in love with her?'

'Well, you're so angry with her.'

Her heart was pumping like a marathon runner's, but she forced herself to continue on lightly, though her hands were curled into tight balls. 'I thought it must be because it's so painful for you to see her marrying someone else.'

'I'm delighted to see her marrying someone else,' he bit out. 'Only not *that* bastard.'

'Oh. Good.'

He wasn't very convincing. She realised the ice she was on was wafer-thin, but, having gone this far, she drew another tentative breath and met his gaze squarely, hoping her desperation and panic didn't swirl in her eyes. 'But you did marry her, Sam. You must have loved her at one stage.'

He stared at her for seconds, his mouth grim, his eyes

glinting in speculation, then took her arm firmly and urged her towards their table. 'It's not Natalie I'm angry with, it's myself. This is not the time and place to discuss it. The sooner we finish our meals, the sooner we can escape.'

He held her chair for her and resumed his own. It was hard to think of eating when the full heart-shattering impact of her insignificance in Sam's scheme of things had only just dawned. Strangely, apart from Irene, who wasn't likely to admit it anyway, she seemed to be the only person in Sam's life who'd never considered, until this weekend, that he might still be in love with his ex. She recalled the first time she'd ever seen Natalie at the office, and the things the peroxide blonde had been screeching.

The signs had been there all along. How could she have missed them?

Thankfully the remains of her meal had been taken away, and she was able to get off lightly with some thin vegetable soup Sam found for her at the buffet. During the lull, a dauntingly groomed billionaire's wife across the table from them leaned forward and said, 'Excuse me, Eleanor…'

'Ellie, please.'

The woman smiled, then indicated Ellie's dress. 'Do you mind if I ask? Is your dress a Dinnigan?'

'Yes.'

'Not Flirty Noir, by any chance?'

She nodded, and the woman sighed, 'How I envy you.'

Even while trawling the depths of despair, there were a few pleasures left to a woman. Sam would probably have forgotten the foul aspersions he'd cast on her dress and her spirited defence of it. Nevertheless, she couldn't resist a subtle sideways glance at him to see if he'd heard. Amazingly, his eyes meshed instantly with hers, brimming with amused comprehension.

Smiling, he set down his glass. 'Excuse me,' he said to their neighbours. 'I have to dance with my fiancée.'

His use of the word cut deep, but she didn't protest. She let him lead her to the dance floor and draw her into his arms. Other dancers were jerking about as single, separate entities, but Sam, being the old-fashioned guy he was, liked to hold a woman close. His long thighs brushed hers, and she inhaled the familiar, masculine scent of him and gave herself up to the impossible torture of being held against the man she loved.

As if to add to her bitter-sweet joy, the band eased into a poignant old love song. Sam steered her through the open doors onto a small circular terrace that had been designed to vaguely resemble a small Venetian temple, and was open to the starry sky. The warm, scented Queensland night, meant for lovers, tormented her senses unbearably.

'Alone at last,' Sam said with a shuddering sigh. His hand slipped under her hair and stroked down her spine, moulding her close to his big, hard body. 'Do you know what torture this is for me?' he murmured, brushing her temple with his jaw. 'Do you have any idea what a living hell I'm in tonight?'

Hot needles of pain lanced her heart. She closed her eyes. 'I think I do.'

There was a hoarseness in his voice, as if he spoke from the very depths of his being. 'Imagine, Eleanor... Imagine knowing you could have been happy with the one person you belong to, who should belong to you, but, like a fool, you ruined all your chances.'

Misery choked her throat. 'I *can* imagine.' The song spilling from the ballroom swelled into its plaintive refrain of tragedy and heartbreak.

His deep voice grew laboured and emotional. 'If you knew...what it means to me to—smell the fragrance of your hair, to feel your soft breasts against my chest...'

She looked up blindly at him. '*My* hair? But I thought you... You know... Natalie.'

'Natalie?' Sam stood stock-still and stared at her, gripping her shoulders. Then he said, very softly and distinctly, 'I married Natalie because she was pregnant. For no other reason. It was my mistake. Then two months after the wedding she was offered the part she longed for in that soap. She chose to get rid of our baby rather than lose her big break.' As he gazed at her his stern, sensuous mouth twisted. 'And most of it was my fault.'

Shock, and the rock-bottom despair so eloquently expressed in Sam's wry unemotional tone, welled in Ellie's heart to join all her own grief and pain and disappointment, and flooded through her in a huge rolling wave. The tears rushed to her eyes and spilled over before she could stop them.

'Don't, *don't.*' Sam's voice was suddenly strained and urgent. He folded her in his arms and pressed her tenderly to him as if she were some piece of rare fragile china, stroking her hair. She could feel the tense emotion racking his big lean body as he murmured passionate endearments. 'Please, please Ellie, my sweetheart. Don't cry.'

For a while she couldn't even speak to deny the charge, and she was grateful when he hustled her back through the hotel, past the glimmering lagoon and up to the Principessa.

The lamps were on, warming the sitting room with their glow. Ellie mopped abjectly at her eyes with a handful of tissues. 'I'm so sorry, Sam,' she said, turning away from him to spare him the ghastly sight. 'I can't imagine what got into me. I'm not usually a weeper. It must have been the—the lobster, or…' She caught sight of her face in a mirror and saw to her horror that her mascara had started to drip.

Sam turned her around to face him and wiped under her eyes with his handkerchief. Sighing, he said, 'I thought—*hoped*—you might be feeling sad about breaking my heart.'

She looked to see if he was joking, but his eyes were darkly serious, intent on her face, the lines around his chiselled mouth taut. She gasped and her wet eyelids fluttered in shock. 'Your—your *heart*, Sam.'

He said hoarsely, 'We both know I'm not good at saying the right words to you, Eleanor. God knows, I've made mistakes. But I have to try one more time to…to somehow *show* you…what's in my heart, what's been in my heart since the first time I saw you on that balcony.' He kept gesturing very emotionally. 'I know I-I've hurt you. I upset your life, plunging you into an affair like a selfish bloody fool. Expecting you to forgive me when…' His hand made a passionate reefing motion through his hair. 'I thought you seemed to—I *hoped* you felt the same way.' He half turned away and said wryly, 'But then I understood it was your career you loved. I felt…'

Her eyes started to swim. 'Oh, no, Sam. No.'

He was gazing at her with the most earnest, and fiercely tender expression in his gorgeous dark eyes. 'You see, my darling Eleanor…'

All at once she had the most thrilling sensation that, against all the odds, the grand and magical moment she'd dreamed of in her wildest fantasies might have arrived. She touched his lean, tanned hand, and, to encourage him, said, 'Ellie, please, Sam.'

His eyebrows lifted and he broke into a laugh. 'Thank God, at last. *Ellie.*'

On his tongue her name sounded so romantic, almost haunting in fact, it was music to her ears.

He took her hands in his firm, warm grip, and grew serious again. 'You need to understand something. It's taken me a while to realise all this myself.' He let go of her hands and gestured his remorse. 'Looking back now, I have to accept most of the responsibility for the disaster with Natalie. When she discovered she was pregnant, I was horrified, to say the least, but I gritted my teeth and pressured her into marriage.' His expression grew very grave. 'In our families, you know, we don't deny our children. I suppose I knew vaguely how serious she was about being an actress, but I was intolerant.' He evaded her eyes and stared down at the floor, shaking his head. 'And as you can imagine, we didn't get on from the start.' He glanced up at her, a wry smile lighting his dark eyes. '*You* should have been there. You could have poured your magic oil. Every day was World War Three.'

Ellie could well imagine it. Volatile Natalie, with an icy cool, controlled Sam. Not a marriage made in heaven.

'Then,' he continued with an apologetic grimace, 'I'm afraid I made it clear that I expected her to give up acting when the child was born, and for several years after. In that industry, as she was always insisting, the opportunities have to be seized when they arise. I suppose she felt trapped.' He sprang up and started to pace restlessly about the room. 'I can never, ever excuse what she did. But lately I can't help wondering if things would have been different if we hadn't married. She'd probably have been happy to be a single working mum, given the chance. But I didn't really give her the chance.' He halted his pacing and stood with his face averted from her, his breathing heavy and painful, his powerful shoulders rigid. With a tortured sideways glance at her he said, very quietly, 'I was gutted when I found out, Ellie. I hadn't realised how much I'd looked forward to it.' He lifted his hand in a sharp, constrained gesture. 'The child.'

A hot, fierce surge of compassion flooded Ellie's heart, and she jumped up from the sofa. 'Oh, Sam,' she said, rushing across to throw her arms around him. 'You did what you thought was right.'

He held her against his chest, then put her a little away from him to frown intently down at her. 'I did, of course, but do you see? When you came home with me that last night I so wanted you to stay, Ellie. But I was afraid that if I put pressure on *you* to—to change your direction so drastically when you love your life the way it is, you would run like the wind.' The rueful grimace he gave tore her heart. 'But then you did, anyway.'

'Oh.' She shook her head in dismayed remorse. 'But I thought... You know, you said you only wanted me for a week, or—or a year...' Her voice started to wobble with the memory of the devastation it had caused her, and Sam drew her back into his strong arms and dragged her against him.

'Shh, shh,' he said, stroking her hair and tenderly kissing her neck. 'Don't cry any more, my love.' Pressed with such passionate tenderness against his warm chest, she felt his deep voice resonate through her. 'I was such a fool. I was so afraid of losing you, I said all the wrong things.'

She drew back to smile at him through the mist. 'What was that you called me? Your *love*?'

'Well, you are my love!' He looked wonderingly at her, and his voice deepened with raw emotion. 'You must know I love you, Ellie. I fell in love with you on that very first night, and then like a fool I let you disappear. But I couldn't forget you. I was crazy to find you. For God's sake, I bought a bloody *bank* to find you! You're the love of my life!'

Fireworks and starbursts were exploding in her heart, but Sam held her from him, a sudden uncertainty dawning in his eyes. 'And you? Do *you*…?'

She said softly, 'I do, Sam. I do love you. I adore you.'

With his dark velvet eyes glowing, he said very solemnly, 'So then, Ellie O'Dea, will you marry me?'

She hesitated. Her heart began to quake with a suffocating fear that caught her entire body in a cold, vicious clench. In a voice toneless with dread she said, 'Sam, there is something I need to tell you.'

He frowned. The shining light in his eyes was doused.

'It's possible—' She braced herself with a deep trembling breath. A blush rose inside her and flooded her all the way to her roots, but for all her faults she had her own code of honour. She met Sam's anxious, uncertain gaze, and forced her chin and voice to stay steady. 'It's quite possible, Sam, that although I would *love* to have your children, it may be difficult for me to conceive. This being the case, you might want to reconsider the idea of marriage to me.'

He let out a long breath and his eyes lit with the most fervent relief. 'Oh, Ellie. My darling Ellie. As if that could make me not want to marry you.' He gazed tenderly at her, his eyes ablaze with concern. 'There are alternatives, you know.

There're…clinics…adoption—' He waved his hands expressively and said very firmly, 'There are options. Let's talk about all that later. You still haven't answered my question.' He captured her hands again in his warm, sure grip. 'Well, my love? Will you?'

An exquisite joy filled her heart to overflowing. 'Yes, Sam. Oh, yes.'

CHAPTER THIRTEEN

BEDS at the Palazzo Versace were exceptionally springy and comfortable. Just supposing a person had time to sleep and was in need of a pillow, there were seven varieties to choose from, each softer and more cushioning than the last.

After her night of sheer heavenly bliss with the most tender and virile lover a woman could ever expect to know, Ellie faced the dawn feeling energised right through to her soul, with her every muscle supple and relaxed.

She felt dreamily ready to embrace the day and take charge of her commitments. The first was the little matter of Natalie's and Michael's disagreement.

When she informed Sam of Natalie's wedding being in doubt, his first response was to yawn. 'Oh, for God's sake. Seriously?'

'I'm afraid so,' she said, lounging beside him in the sumptuous bed, enjoying the warmth and support of his gorgeous bronzed chest. 'Poor Natalie. After everyone's gone to so much trouble. What a shame if, at the end of all this, she's still Natalie Stilakos.'

She slanted a glance up at him, and noted, with some satisfaction, horror dawning on his stubbly morning face.

'Bloody hell,' he exclaimed with heartfelt fervour. 'What's it all about, anyway?'

She snuggled up to him. 'Oh, I don't know. Something about Michael wanting someone to forgive him for something he's done in the past. He's all depressed about it. You know how these things can fester.'

There was a heavy impenetrable silence, then he bit out softly, 'Some things are unforgivable.'

'Yes.' She sighed. 'I know.'

After a small lapse he said, 'What do you know?'

'I agree with you. Some things can't be forgiven.'

He enquired with what sounded like difficulty, 'Are you referring to the way I hurt you—the things that happened about your job? Or the other things. The things I told you about with Natalie.'

She arched her brows and said airily, 'No, no, no. I was merely making the point that while *things* can't always be forgiven, people can. Especially when you're happy.'

He smiled down at her for a moment, and whispered, 'I'm happy.' Then the smile grew sinful and his eyes lascivious, and he planted a greedy kiss on her bare shoulder.

Eventually she was free to deal with Natalie and the dress, which turned out to be a magnificently beaded sheath, with a fish tail to the ground, shimmering with sequins in blue, silver and pinky mauve. She managed to squeeze into most of it, although, as Natalie had predicted, the bust was a little in need of letting out. Fortunately her parents could summon seamstresses from afar at will, and did so without hesitation.

While the fitting was going on, she happened to glance out of Natalie's window, and with a pleased little glow saw Sam, strolling towards a table beside the lagoon, deep in conversation with his cousin. Michael seemed to be doing lots of fast talking, while Sam had that stern, listening demeanour she'd experienced on a few occasions herself.

After the fitting, and satisfied she wouldn't look any worse than the average rainbow trout, she allowed Natalie to sweep her off to the Palazzo beauty parlour, where she was pampered, manicured, waxed, painted and perfumed like a sultan's courtesan. Inspired by the fish frock, she opted for a return to her pale strawberry hair, ensuring it was more on the blonde side this time than the pink. She submitted to it all with enjoyment, thinking with a deep, joyous excitement of the magic night to come.

All the magic nights. Sam would appreciate it as thoroughly as any sultan.

Natalie's wedding was a romantic, twilit event. A Persian carpet, scattered with frangipani and flanked by hundreds of lights, was laid on the sand for the wedding party. An enormous marquee spread with more exotic carpets and big soft cushions, was provided for the guests to lounge upon like Arabian potentates. Dozens of security guards had been employed to hold back the sea of media cameras.

The bride looked beautiful in a diamond-and-pearl encrusted dress, with a veil and train worth millions, that was reminiscent of hanging seaweed. Michael wore a long white embroidered shirt-frock affair over his trousers. Ellie couldn't see that it was very fishy, but it was dignified, at least.

Ellie did her part gravely, walking barefoot behind Natalie along the Persian, in her beautiful fish frock and mermaid's hair. Though most people's attention was on the bride and groom, whenever Ellie looked at Sam, he was smiling at her.

When it came time to kiss the bride, Sam strode over to swing Ellie off the ground and kiss her, then a beaming Irene dashed over to kiss and violently hug her as well. While the wedding barbecues and bonfires were lit, and people plunged into the party, Sam held Ellie's hand and walked with her along the beach. And while the festivities raged on into the night, Sam took her up to the Principessa and made passionate love with her till dawn.

'Is Ellie always this cool, calm and collected, Sam?' a friend queried the next day, when Ellie and Sam were lazing by the lagoon, wrapped in blissful contemplation of each other.

'Not always,' Sam said, pausing in taking a sip from Ellie's straw to gaze meditatively at her. ' I think I may have seen her get a little frayed around the edges, once or twice.'

Their smiling eyes met.

Don't miss favorite author

Michelle Reid's

next book, coming in May 2008,
brought to you only
by Harlequin Presents!

THE MARKONOS BRIDE

#2723

Aristos is bittersweet for Louisa: here, she met
and married gorgeous Greek playboy Andreas
Markonos and produced a precious son. After
tragedy, Louisa was compelled to leave.
Five years later, she is back....

*Look out for more spectacular stories
from Michelle Reid, coming soon in 2008!*

HARLEQUIN *Presents*

Look out for brilliant author

Susan Napier

in May 2008—
only in Harlequin Presents!

ACCIDENTAL MISTRESS
#2729

One night Emily Quest is rescued by a handsome
stranger. Despite the heart–stopping attraction
between them, Emily thought she'd never see
him again. But now, years later, he is right in front
of her, as sexy as ever....

*Don't miss Susan's next book in Harlequin
Presents—coming soon!*

HARLEQUIN *Presents*

Don't forget Harlequin Presents EXTRA
now brings you a powerful new collection
every month featuring four books!

Be sure not to miss any of the titles in

In the Greek Tycoon's Bed,
available May 13:

THE GREEK'S
FORBIDDEN BRIDE
by Cathy Williams

THE GREEK TYCOON'S
UNEXPECTED WIFE
by Annie West

THE GREEK TYCOON'S
VIRGIN MISTRESS
by Chantelle Shaw

THE GIANNAKIS BRIDE
by Catherine Spencer

REQUEST YOUR FREE BOOKS!

 HARLEQUIN® *Presents*~ ®

PASSION GUARANTEED SEDUCTION

2 FREE NOVELS PLUS 2
FREE GIFTS!

YES! Please send me 2 FREE Harlequin Presents® novels and my 2 FREE gifts (gifts are worth about $10). After receiving them, if I don't wish to receive any more books, I can return the shipping statement marked "cancel". If I don't cancel, I will receive 6 brand-new novels every month and be billed just $4.05 per book in the U.S. or $4.74 per book in Canada, plus 25¢ shipping and handling per book and applicable taxes, if any*. That's a savings of close to 15% off the cover price! I understand that accepting the 2 free books and gifts places me under no obligation to buy anything. I can always return a shipment and cancel at any time. Even if I never buy another book, the two free books and gifts are mine to keep forever.   106 HDN ERRW 306 HDN ERRL

Name   (PLEASE PRINT)

Address   Apt. #

City   State/Prov.   Zip/Postal Code

Signature (if under 18, a parent or guardian must sign)

Mail to the **Harlequin Reader Service:**
IN U.S.A.: P.O. Box 1867, Buffalo, NY 14240-1867
IN CANADA: P.O. Box 609, Fort Erie, Ontario L2A 5X3

Not valid to current subscribers of Harlequin Presents books.

Want to try two free books from another line?
Call 1-800-873-8635 or visit www.morefreebooks.com.

* Terms and prices subject to change without notice. N.Y. residents add applicable sales tax. Canadian residents will be charged applicable provincial taxes and GST. This offer is limited to one order per household. All orders subject to approval. Credit or debit balances in a customer's account(s) may be offset by any other outstanding balance owed by or to the customer. Please allow 4 to 6 weeks for delivery. Offer available while quantities last.

Your Privacy: Harlequin Books is committed to protecting your privacy. Our Privacy Policy is available online at www.eHarlequin.com or upon request from the Reader Service. From time to time we make our lists of customers available to reputable third parties who may have a product or service of interest to you. If you would prefer we not share your name and address, please check here. ☐

HP08

Inside ROMANCE

Stay up-to-date on all your romance reading news!

Inside Romance is a FREE quarterly newsletter highlighting our upcoming series releases and promotions.

Visit

www.eHarlequin.com/InsideRomance

to sign up to receive our complimentary newsletter today!

TALL, DARK AND SEXY

The men who never fail—seduction included!

Brooding, successful and arrogant, these men
can sweep any female they desire off her feet.
But now there's only one woman they want—
and they'll use their wealth, power, charm and
irresistibly seductive ways to claim her!

**Don't miss any of the titles in this exciting
collection available June 10, 2008:**

*Harlequin Presents EXTRA delivers a themed
collection every month featuring 4 new titles.*